To Trish
(for getting there!)

1

Whenever I hear the word *auction* I think of dusty timelessness and of sad things that were once loved by people now dead. But most of all I think of Maria Smythe and that weird summer of chilling events. Normally you wouldn't find me in a stuffy old auction room. Normally I'd be hanging out with my mates, perfecting some rollerblade moves or playing computer games. But most of them had been hauled away on holidays. So I was stuck at home with just my cousin Susy for company. She'd been sent to stay with us while her parents were in Scotland. I could understand why they wouldn't want to take a bossy busybody like her with them, but did they have to unload her on us?

It was Dad who'd suggested that we tag along with him.

'Come to the auction with me, you two,' he said. 'You might pick up some useful tips.'

'Yecchh,' I said. I wasn't all that pushed about my parents' antique shop. So long as it made enough money to finance a life of relative comfort and trendy gear for me, it was okay. Just don't ask me to get excited

5

about fiddly tables with curly legs or Victorian prints of sighing maidens and whiskery old fogies.

Needless to say, Susy hopped up and down like a mad flea at the invitation, her flaming hair bouncing. She'd never been to an auction. All the way there in the car she kept asking Dad daft questions.

'If I sneeze will the auctioneer think I'm bidding? Do people wave little cards, like in the movies? Will there be amazingly valuable stuff with people bidding by phone from Japan and America?'

Dad laughed. 'Hold on there, lady,' he said. 'It's just a country auction. Mostly junk, but one can get lucky.'

He was right. It was a load of gloomy paintings of dreary landscapes and really ugly people, cracked china ornaments and wormy sideboards. It was so boring my brain got *rigor mortis*. 'Will this take much longer?' I whispered to Dad a million hours later.

'Sshh,' he replied, without taking his eyes off the auctioneer. 'Near the end now.'

'Lot number one hundred and twenty-four,' began the droning auctioneer, mopping his domed forehead. One hundred and twenty-four! Had I really stuck it here through that number of junk items and remained sane? The porter was holding up a couple of dusty old sketchbooks, the sort that art students haul around with them.

'A set of paintings and sketches by...' the auctioneer pushed his glasses along his nose and peered at his list, '...by Maria Smythe.' He paused. 'All original work,' he said. 'Could be worth a lot of money.'

'Oh, I'd love to have those,' said Susy. 'Could I bid for them, Frank?' She looked pleadingly at Dad. 'I have a fiver.' He shrugged his shoulders and smiled at her.

'No harm in having a go,' he said. 'Wait until someone starts the bidding.'

'It's just a load of rubb...' I began, then ducked out of range of Susy's bony knuckles. You don't mess with Susy when she gets an idea. As it happened, nobody was interested in the dusty old sketchbooks, so they were knocked down to Susy for three quid.

'What about that, then?' she gloated. 'I've bid at an auction!'

Waste of money, I thought. But I had the good sense to say nothing. It was then, as the porter put the sketchbooks on a side table, that I saw the girl in the blue dress.

She was standing at the table where the porter had left Susy's tatty sketchbooks, riffling through them with a sort of anxious desperation. Then she turned and looked straight at me. Cheek, I thought, suddenly protective, even though I figured Susy had been taken for a sucker.

'Someone poking about your property,' I said to Susy.

'What?'

I nodded towards the table where the girl had been, but she was gone.

'Nerd,' muttered Susy. 'There's nobody at my stuff. You're winding me up. Pathetic.'

'Well, there was someone at them,' I went on. 'A girl with long fair hair down to her waist. And she was wearing a blue dress with a ribbon around her waist and frilly things down the front.'

'Huh,' scoffed Susy. 'Who in their right mind would wear gear like that? Maybe it was Alice in Wonderland who took a wrong turn. You're hallucinating. Comes from eating too much chocolate – it addles weak brains.'

'Oh, suit yourself,' I said, and went over to help Dad load his junk into the back of the car. I kept a lookout for the girl in the blue dress, but she didn't reappear. Perhaps Susy was right. Perhaps I'd been in a catatonic state from boredom and had imagined that figure. But, whether imagination or reality, she was stamped on my mind. Something about the way she'd looked at me.

Mum reacted with a gasp when Susy

gleefully showed her the sketchbooks later.

'Bid for them all by myself,' said Susy.

'Bet the auctioneer was glad to get rid of them,' I said. 'Saw you for a sucker straight away. Three quid for a few scrawls!' It was safe to say all that now. Susy wouldn't strangle me in front of Mum.

There were several sketches of an old geezer in working clothes, some detailed drawings of trees and plants, but it was the drawings of an old house that excited Mum.

'For heaven's sake!' she exclaimed as she smoothed them out on the floor of the living room. 'These are pictures of the old Smythe place, Heather Grange.'

'You know this house, Una?' said Susy.

'Know it!' laughed Mum. 'I used to cycle there with my pals as a kid. It's about three miles out. It's the eeriest old house you could imagine, at the end of a long avenue.'

Mum had grown up locally. In fact the antique shop had once been her father's grocery store and we lived above it in her old home. I looked with fresh interest at the house drawings. They were dated 1930 and signed *Maria Smythe aged twelve*. What strange obsession had made this girl, about my own age, draw this spooky house over and over? And why was that odd-looking girl at the auction so interested in them?

Later on, long after midnight, I jumped awake when my light was switched on.

'Susy,' I groaned. 'It's half-past three. What do you think you're at?'

Susy was standing motionless at the door. Her face was deathly pale.

'That girl,' she whispered.

'What girl? What are you on about?'

'The one you saw at the auction,' she put in. She walked over to my bed and peered at me intently. There's heavy stuff coming when Susy peers. 'With the weird gear.'

'What about her?' I asked.

'Tell me what she was like.'

'Is that all?' I snorted. 'At this hour of the night you wake me up to ask me about ...'

'Tell me,' Susy insisted.

Something in her voice and expression stopped me in mid-insult.

'I told you,' I said. 'Blue dress and a ribbon thing.'

'And frills down the front?' said Susy.

I nodded. My cousin was mad. You're supposed to humour mad people. 'Yeah, Susy. Frills down the front.'

Susy sat on the edge of my bed. 'She was in my room. Just now. She was in my room.'

2

Neither of us mentioned Susy's so-called visitor next morning at breakfast. Susy was strangely quiet. As far as I was concerned she had had a bad dream – probably prompted by the excitement of her first big business venture for three quid. But her white face and sunken eyes told me that she hadn't slept much.

'Fancy you finding those sketchbooks, Susy,' Mum said. 'I only ever remember that house as a ruin. It's interesting to see pictures of it in its former glory.'

'What do you know about that old house?' I asked Mum. 'Heather Grange.'

'Not a lot,' said Mum. 'Like I said, it was always a ruin in my time. People said it was haunted. There was some sort of a story, though,' she continued.

'Story? What kind of story?' I asked.

Mum wrinkled her brow as she tried to remember. 'Something about a tragedy.'

At that, Susy perked up. 'Tragedy?'

Mum nodded. 'Oh, you know how silly rumours grow up around an old place.'

'Rumours?' Susy leaned towards Mum.

Mum shrugged. 'Just the usual stories they tell about old houses. You know.'

'I don't know,' Susy said impatiently. 'What stories?'

'Oh, foul deeds, someone disappearing, that sort of thing. Like I said, just rumours.'

'Wow!' I was impressed. Now we were getting somewhere. 'Deadly. Tell us more.'

Mum shrugged again and began gathering up the breakfast things. 'Well, it was probably the power of suggestion, but nobody ever went beyond the inner gate at the end of that avenue.'

'Why not?' I persisted.

'It was said that something evil lurked beyond that point. Silly, but it put the fear of God into a bunch of youngsters.'

'Did you go beyond the inner gate?'

Mum shook her head. 'Not me,' she said. 'That place used to freak me out. I always stayed on this side of the gate, firmly pointed towards the road.'

'You were a wimp then,' I said.

'Your original cowardly wimp. And I lived to tell the tale. There was no way you'd get me to climb over that gate.'

'I wish you'd tell me more about the house, Mum.'

Mum set about putting the butter and stuff in the fridge. 'I've told you, Arty,' she said. 'There's nothing more to tell. Maybe Mrs Powell could tell you more. She was born here way before my time. Why don't you ask her and not be tormenting me? Now, hurry up, I've to get down to the shop.'

Mrs Powell is an incredibly old lady who lives in what's politely called a retirement residence, but that's really just a posh name for the old folks' home in a converted Georgian house at the edge of our town, Cashelderry. That means the castle of the oak wood, but the castle is just a crumbling ruin and the oak wood has been replaced by a shopping centre.

Before my granny died she used to visit Mrs Powell. It seems they were friends way back when cavemen roamed. Now Mum does the visiting bit, and she hauls me along as well. I don't usually hang out with old fogies, but Mrs Powell is a lot of fun. For a wrinkled old bird she packs a neat line of stories and can talk about things that I like. She'd lived abroad for years but came back when she got old. She'd wink and say, 'Lived well and spent well. That's why I'm nearly broke.'

'Good idea,' I said. 'I'll ask Mrs Powell. She won't fob me off with foggy memories.'

'Oh, for heaven's sake, Arty,' Susy burst out. 'Can't you drop this old house thing. Drop it, will you!'

I glanced at Mum. She raised her eyebrows. 'I'll leave you two to finish up here,' she said. 'Got to open the shop.'

I waited until I heard her going downstairs before turning on Susy.

'What's eating you?' I asked. 'You're going mental, you know. First of all you come to my room in the early hours, rabbitting on about someone in your room. And now you're being thorny and rude to me and Mum. Bet I know what it is. Bet you're peed off because you threw three quid down the sewer by buying those stupid sketchbooks. That's what's bugging you, isn't it?'

Susy looked at me scornfully.

'You know nothing,' she scoffed.

'What's that supposed to mean?' I asked.

'You keep going on and on about that house,' she went on. 'And that's what that girl was looking at last night.'

'Oh come on, Susy. Bad dream, that's all.'

But Susy was shaking her head. 'I'm telling you, that girl was in my room and she was looking at the sketchbooks.'

I followed her up to her room, wondering if her brand of insanity was hereditary. With a dramatic sweep, she opened her door.

'Look,' she said.

Scattered around the floor were the sketchbooks she'd bought yesterday. They were all open.

I snorted. 'You're blaming a total stranger for your messiness... Sure, Susy. She broke in here in the middle of the night just to throw a few grotty drawings around. Get real.'

But Susy was shaking her head. 'I never touched them,' she said. 'And I never tore out those pages. I woke up long after everyone had gone to bed. The room was cold, like a fridge. Then I heard the rustle of paper over on the table where I'd left the sketchbooks. At first I thought it was you up to some of you nerdy tricks – scribbling on the drawings or something ...'

'Thanks a bunch,' I put in.

Susy ignored my remark. 'But in the light from the landing I could see it was a girl. She was kneeling on the floor, and she was turning the pages of the sketchbooks. I froze, just sat in bed watching her. She looked ...' Susy paused, a faraway look in her eyes.

'She looked what?' I said. 'Come on, Susy. You're having me on.'

'No, Arty, I'm not. I'm telling you the gospel truth. You've got to believe me.'

The way she said it made me shiver. 'Go on,' I said meekly. 'She looked what?'

'She looked sort of frantic.'

'Frantic?'

'Yes. It was as if she was looking for some-thing. It was scary, I can tell you.'

'And then?' I prompted.

Susy shrugged. 'Then nothing. I must have made a sound – she looked straight at me and then just disappeared.'

'Disappeared?' I tried not to laugh. This had gone beyond scary; we were into total loopiness now.

Susy frowned. 'I know you're thinking I'm a nutter,' she said. 'But I'm telling you, Arty, it's true. All of it. Have a look at the drawings that she was looking at.'

'It's the house,' I said. 'She's turned out the drawings of the house.'

Susy was nodding in agreement. 'Do you think she was trying to tell me something?' she asked. 'I've looked and looked at those drawings, but I can't see anything odd.'

I still wasn't convinced. However, I was game for a bit of intrigue, if there was any.

'Why don't we cycle to the old place?' I said. 'It's only a couple of miles away.'

Susy brightened. 'Could we?' she said. 'That would be deadly.'

'Might see your frilly night visitor,' I sniggered.

That visit was to trigger events that neither of us could have imagined.

3

'Bet there's nothing spooky about the place,' I said. 'Mum and her lot were just a bunch of seventies wallies. Wait and see.'

The tall chimneys of the house were barely visible from the road. It *did* look spooky, but I wasn't about to admit this to Susy.

'Well, what are we waiting for?' she said. 'Let's go.'

We shoved our bikes into the long grass and headed through a gap in the bars of the big rusty gates that hung crookedly from crumbling piers. Maybe it was Susy's white-faced determination, maybe it was the feeling of isolation now that we'd arrived at this place, that made me want to back off. I gritted my teeth and kept telling myself that Susy had simply dreamt about that girl based on my description of her at the auction.

But a nagging pulse at the back of my brain reminded me that my feisty cousin was not given to hysterical imaginings. And it was that thought that made me point to the notice that was nailed to a tree.

'No trespassing,' I read, with badly disguised relief. 'The sign says 'No...'

'I can read,' Susy retorted. 'Don't mind that. There's probably a man with thousands of those signs who just wanders around the country looking for spots to nail them to. They don't mean a thing.'

She turned and looked at me, frowning and grinning at the same time.

'You're not scared, are you?'

'Huh, as if.' I hoped she wouldn't notice that my voice had gone up several decibels.

We hacked our way through the high weeds that choked what must have once been a sweeping avenue. The trees on either side made that sort of whispering sound that would freak you out if you were alone.

'This is a daft idea,' I said, with as much authority as I could muster. Which wasn't much. 'Nettles and thistles and a tumble-down old hovel. Come on, Susy, we could get our swimming gear and head for the pool in town. Have a Coke after and hang out in the shopping centre ...'

'Naw. This was a brilliant idea of yours, Arty.' She beamed at me. I've never met any-one who can do quick-change expressions like Susy. She can cut through metal with a look one minute and charm unsuspecting victims to their knees the next. 'Totally brilliant,' she added, big eyes on full power.

I knew that was just blatant flattery, but I

fell for it and continued hacking through the thorny jungle. Rounding a bend we came suddenly on the house.

'Wow!' we both said together. It certainly was big. And silent. Well, you'd expect silence from a house with no people in it, but if it could have a colour, this silence would be black. The front had long windows with lots of small panes. They were firmly shuttered. The door was boarded up with planks of wood. Long grass whispered all around, and the lonely coo of wood pigeons added to the desolate atmosphere.

'Keaaghh, keaaghh.'

Susy and I jumped.

'Only crows,' I said, as a bunch of the screeching things flew up from the trees. I hoped Susy couldn't hear my heart thumping the scared thump of a coward. Not that it mattered; I could tell her own heart was on overdrive. If she had a heart, that is.

'Hell,' she said with a nervous laugh. 'Nearly did for me, the stupid things.'

When I'd extracted her nails from my arm, I fished a folded-up drawing from my pocket.

'You brought one of the drawings!' said Susy. 'Why didn't I think of that?'

'Because I'm the one with the brains, kid. Just keep remembering that.'

'Huh,' said Susy, trying to sound scornful.

That didn't cut any ice, considering she'd nearly amputated my arm.

'Look at this,' I went on, pointing to the drawing and then at the house. 'Something fishy here.'

Susy looked over my shoulder. We looked at the drawing in silence for a few moments.

'It's the roof,' Susy then said. 'See? In the picture there's an attic window on the roof.'

'You're right,' I said. 'There's no sign of it now.' Sure enough, where there was a meticulously drawn attic window in the sketch, that area was now tiled over with slates.

'She must have made a mistake,' put in Susy. 'This Maria what's-her-name must have made a mistake by putting in an attic window that doesn't exist.'

'But everything else in the drawing is so carefully detailed, right down to the moulded designs on the chimneys. Why would she get the roof wrong?'

Susy looked again at the drawing.

'You could be right,' she muttered. 'There must be some reason why that window no longer exists. Let's mooch around and see what we can find.'

'You're not going in?' I spluttered. 'There could be some maniac in there who'd take a shot at us for trespassing.'

'That's you all over, isn't it, Arty? You're

just a wimp. I'm going in.'

'Who's calling who a wimp?' I protested, but Susy was barging ahead. I followed her over the gate, the one that Mum had mentioned – the inner gate. As we neared the house we instinctively moved closer together. From a distance it had been big, but from close up it was awesome. The seven upstairs windows seemed to be watching us. Waiting.

'Creepy,' I said, swallowing hard so that my voice wouldn't come out as a squeak.

The planks across the front door were very crudely held together. Very easy to prise away, I thought. Why hadn't someone done that ages ago? But then, Mum had said that no-body would venture beyond the inner gate.

'What do you say we pull those planks away and have a look inside?' said Susy.

'You've got to be kidding,' I said. 'That's breaking and entering.' By now I was bitterly regretting my great idea of coming here. My idea of winding Susy up had gone sour.

'You watch too many police dramas, Arty.' said Susy. 'All jargon and no guts. What harm can it be just to look around?'

I expelled an exasperated breath. 'Don't blame me if we're hauled up in court.'

We discovered that one of the door panels was missing, leaving just enough room for two skinny kids like us to get through.

'You first,' said Susy. Typical. There was nothing for it but to see this thing through or else be branded as a chicken-livered wally for the rest of my life. I took a deep breath and squeezed through the narrow gap. The strong smell of must and decay made me gasp. When my eyes got used to the gloom, I took in the enormous hall. Where I was standing there were patterned tiles which had become grubby with age and neglect. On the right and left there were two panelled doors, both closed. Farther down the hall there was a wide arch with tattered curtains held back on either side. Beyond the arch an imposing staircase curved up to a railed landing where a high, stained-glass window let in beams of dusty light.

As I gazed hypnotically at the spirals of multi-coloured dust, they suddenly dispersed as if a gust of wind had disturbed them. But there was no wind; it was a calm summer's day. The light faded and the hall became dark. It wasn't so much the lack of light that freaked me – I put that down to a cloud passing over the sun. No, it was the awful sense of a presence other than my own. Someone watching. Every nerve was poised for standby flight. And then I heard a sound that unlocked my trance. A soft, echoing whistle.

'Susy! That's not funny!' I turned. Her moon face was framed in the broken panel.

She put a shoulder through to follow me inside. The sudden sight of her blocking the only way out caused me to panic.

'Get out!' I screamed, pushing her roughly. 'Out!' Through my terror I could vaguely hear that whistling sound again. I forced my way after her. In my mad rush I got firmly stuck.

'Susy!' I croaked, 'Susy, pull me out!'

Susy picked herself up, brushed her knees and gave me a filthy look.

'I will in my eye,' she replied.

'Susy!' I was screaming now. 'There's something pulling me. Susy!' Some force was pulling me back into that awful hallway, like an invisible fist pulling my back pocket. I struggled to keep my head and shoulders outside the door. 'Please, Susy!' I cried.

She made a face. I could tell she thought that this was another one of my funky tricks. But the more she heaved the greater became the force of whatever was holding me.

'You might co-operate a tad, Arty,' Susy grunted. 'Push yourself.'

'I'm trying,' I gasped. 'Come on, Susy, get your back into it.'

With a final heave, I fell out on to the

gravel. Tears flowed down my face. I felt the side of my body that had been trapped and could hardly believe the icy cold that emanated from every pore.

'Let's get out of here,' I shouted, willing my trembling knees to point me in the direction of home. Neither of us spoke as we charged through the brambles and nettles, ignoring the stings and scratches.

'What was all that about?' Susy asked as we scrabbled in the long grass for our bikes.

'Didn't you feel it?' I panted. 'Didn't you feel that there was something there?'

'What are you talking about? If there was anything there it was probably a family of mice scared stiff by your lump of a body invading their space.'

'In the hall,' I went on, glancing fearfully back at the house as we made our way to the main gate. 'Didn't you feel that...that dark presence in the hall?'

Susy spluttered and gave me a disbelieving grin. 'Give over, Arty,' she said. 'Next you'll be telling me that Mulder and Scully from "The X-Files" are on their way. Get real.'

Here was a turnaround. *I'd* been the one scoffing at *her* for her spooky interest in this old place; now I was the one freaking out.

'No, it's true, Susy. I swear it's true. Look, let me show you.' I thrust the arm that had

24

been trapped in the hall under her nose. 'Feel that. Feel the cold.'

'So?' she shrugged. 'It's a bit cool. Probably from having your circulation cut off by being jammed in that door.'

'Now feel the other arm,' I said.

Susy snorted. 'Can't say feeling your manky arms is high on my list of things to do,' she began.

'Feel,' I insisted. She squeezed my other arm. 'There, can't you feel the difference?'

'Sure,' said Susy. 'One was washed in new blue Daz, the other in a cheaper detergent.'

'Susy! I'm serious. Something cold was pulling me when I was stuck in that door. You've got to believe me. I'm not taking the mick, honest. I could feel this ... this ...'

'Presence!' snorted Susy. 'You sound like someone in a cheapo movie. Presence, ha!'

'It's the only way I could describe it,' I said, shivering at the memory. 'Something made a sort of whistling sound and tried to pull me back into that place. I'm not telling you a lie.' I was desperate to convince her but I knew that, no matter what I said, Susy would think I was up to my old tricks and that I was just winding her up.

We rode away. I took deep breaths and could feel my body beginning to return to normal. At least I'd stopped shaking.

'Want to come and hang out at the shopping centre?' Susy asked.

'No,' I replied. My head was still a bit messed. I needed time to resurrect myself. 'You go on. See you later back at the house. And, Susy...' She turned.

'Yeah?'

'What about that ... that girl you said you saw in your room last night?'

'I keep telling myself that it was just a dream. Like you said. Anyway, I don't even want to think about it. And that's what you should do too, Arty. All that stuff about something in the hall – it's just your imagination working overtime. Forget it.'

I put my hand on the saddle and twisted around to watch her cycle away, overcome by a sudden feeling of isolation. A feeling that the presence back at that house hadn't really let go of me completely. Turning back, my hand brushed off the back pocket of my jeans. Ripped! As if someone had actually been pulling at the pocket, looking for something. But what? All that was there was a sketch of the house.

The sketch! Was that it? Was that what that thing was after? The blood emptied from my head, like water down a plug-hole.

'Susy!' I called hoarsely, waving the sketch. But she was already out of earshot.

4

That evening, after tea, we went to see Mrs Powell. Susy insisted on coming too. I hadn't really wanted her along because I prefer to talk to Mrs Powell alone. But Susy dug her heels in.

'They're my sketchbooks,' she'd said. 'If you're going to find out about the house that's in my sketchbooks, then I've a right to know too. Besides, I like Mrs Powell. I haven't seen her for ages and I know she adores me.'

'Sometimes her brain doesn't work,' I said, by way of knocking that idle boast.

'What's your problem, Arty?' asked Mum. 'Mrs Powell will be delighted. Her memory comes and goes – she's very old – but she loves company.'

There was no arguing with a couple of viragos, so I just snorted and gave in.

Mrs Powell was sitting in the conservatory, her thin, wrinkled hands folded on the pink blanket that covered her legs.

'Hi, Mrs Powell,' I said.

Her face lit up like a light had gone on inside her head. I suppose I do have that effect on people. Some are born with charm; I guess I'm just one of the lucky ones.

'Well, if it isn't my good friend,' Mrs Powell laughed. 'Come, sit down and annoy me. They're all so nice they make me sick.'

I pulled up a stool and parked myself near her good ear.

'I have my cousin Susy with me,' I said. Not adding that Susy was outside nicking flowers before coming in.

'Susy?' I wished Miss Susy was there to see that she was just a vague memory for the old lady.

'I want to ask you something,' I began, getting straight to the point.

Mrs Powell smiled. 'Anything, lad.'

'Mum said that you know everything about this town. Historical stuff. Right?'

She nodded. 'I lived here even before your granny's time, before I went abroad. I've always loved Cashelderry – that's why I came back two years ago. I want my bones buried here.'

'Don't talk about being buried, Mrs Powell. Make it to a hundred. Then you'll get money from the president and we can both go on a binge.'

She laughed. 'I don't think I want to hang about that long. Now, what do you want to know?'

'There's an old house,' I began. 'A spooky old place that belonged to a family called Smythe.' I fished the now tatty sketch out of my pocket and smoothed it out on my lap. Then I held it where Mrs Powell could see it. Her expression changed. The light in her eyes clouded over and she looked at me anxiously. With a shaky hand, she pushed the drawing away as if the sight of it offended her.

'Hi, Mrs Powell. Here are some flowers.'

I swore under my breath. Trust Susy to breeze in at a crucial moment.

Mrs Powell gladly switched her attention. 'Why it's Susy! How big you've grown.'

Obviously Susy's face had sparked the old lady's memory, so I hadn't even the satisfaction of watching Susy being deflated. As they chatted away, I fidgeted.

'About that house,' I put in during a lull in the mushy talk. Mrs Powell looked at me.

'What about it?' she said softly. 'Why do you want to know about that house?'

'You do know it then?' I said, smoothing out the drawing again.

She looked out of the window at a couple of old people who were choking the birds with stale buns and rasher rinds. A bee buzzed near the open window, changed its mind about coming in, and flew away again.

'That house,' I prompted. 'Are you still

with me, Mrs Powell?'

She turned towards me. 'I'm right with you, lad. Just remembering, that's all.'

'So, what do you remember?'

Susy patted the old lady's hand. 'Leave it, Arty,' she hissed. 'We've had enough of that stupid house for one day.'

Mrs Powell frowned, as if she was struggling to put the words together. I'd never seen her like this before. Mum says that she is a very erudite and articulate lady, which means that she knows heaps of things and can talk a lot. Except that lately her mind sometimes shuts down. Mum said it was because she was worried about her money running out. That sort of stress makes old people's minds go funny.

'The Smythes,' she began eventually. I let out my breath. We were back in business. 'They were a wealthy family. They had one little girl, Maria. I used to know that little girl,' she went on. 'So long ago, I knew her.'

'So what happened to her and her family? Why is the house empty all these years?'

Mrs Powell sighed. 'It was all so tragic,' she said. 'It shouldn't have been so tragic.'

'What happened? What's the tragic bit?'

'Let me tell the story as it comes to me.' She gave me another one of her looks. 'Indulge an old lady and stop interrupting.'

Strange, I thought. At first she'd almost clammed up when I mentioned the house, but now she seemed anxious to talk.

'Mrs Powell,' Susy took the old lady's hand again. 'That girl, Maria.'

Mrs Powell nodded.

'Did she have long hair?'

'For heaven's sake, Susy!' I spluttered. 'They all had long hair back then.'

Susy ignored me. 'Long fair hair,' she went on, her eyes focused intently on Mrs Powell's face. 'Did she have a blue dress? One with frills down the front and a white ribbon around the waist?'

Mrs Powell went a paler shade of her usual white colour and she seemed shaken.

'You've seen photos?' she asked.

Susy shook her head. Mrs Powell made a funny mewing sort of noise.

'Even if I had seen photos, Mrs Powell,' Susy said quietly, 'they wouldn't have been in colour, would they?'

'Oh dear God!' Mrs Powell sagged back in her chair. 'It shouldn't have happened.'

'What do you mean?' Susy asked.

Mrs Powell shook her head slowly and let out a sigh. 'It shouldn't have happened.'

'Mrs Powell?'

Mrs Powell blinked and looked at me. She hadn't answered my question but I didn't push it in case she'd clam up altogether. There was a faraway look in her eyes.

'That James,' she said, with a note of bitterness. 'That James.'

'Who was he? A brother?' I asked. She ignored my question again.

'Drawing. Always drawing. Poor Maria.'

Then she frowned and looked from me to Susy with frightening intensity. Her face was sad, as if a shadow had fallen on it. 'You must stay away from that house, both of you. You must not go there. Do you hear what I'm saying? Stay away from it.' Her gaze wandered to the window again, as if she was depending on the garden to shut out whatever was upsetting her. I waited for her to go on. And waited. Susy continued to hold Mrs Powell's hand. Typical. I just wanted to know what had happened to turn the house into a spooky ruin?

Suddenly Mrs Powell began to gasp.

'Get someone,' she whispered hoarsely. 'Quickly, get someone.'

'Oh God, Mrs Powell!' Susy cried. 'Don't mess around, Arty, do something!'

Mrs Powell reached out and clutched my arm with a panicky grip. This was for real. I jumped up and scarpered down the polished tiles. 'Help!' I shouted. 'Someone, help!'

There was a clatter and a young woman in

a white coat rushed out from a room.

'What is it? What's wrong?'

'Mrs Powell,' I gasped. 'She's gone funny. Quickly, get a doctor.'

'I am a doctor,' replied the woman as she whizzed past me. Within moments there was a team of people with ER-type machines fussing about Mrs Powell. Susy and I stood awkwardly at the far end of the conservatory, not knowing quite what to do. Finally one of the team looked in our direction.

'It's okay, you two,' he said. 'Everything's under control. No point in hanging about.'

'Will she be all right?' Susy asked.

'Yeah. We'll sort her out. Go home now.'

Very soberly Susy and I crept down the avenue. It wasn't until we were on the pavement outside home that we spoke.

'Arty, was it us?' Susy asked.

'Was what us?'

'Did we cause her to go all funny?'

I shrugged. 'Don't know,' I muttered.

'Oh God,' said Susy again. 'If she dies ...'

'She won't die,' I said. 'She's a tough lady. She'll pull through.'

I hoped she would. How could I live with myself if she died because of some awful memory that Susy and I had brought up?

'Was it the house?' asked Susy. 'Or was it the girl?'

'Both, I think,' I replied. No point in each of us blaming the other. 'The two things are mixed up.' I stopped and looked at Susy. 'So, you don't think it was a dream you had last night, then?'

Susy gave a slight shiver. 'Dead sure it wasn't. I knew when Mrs Powell went on about that Maria that it had to be the same girl.'

'Why?'

'Just a hunch,' went on Susy. 'Like you said, the drawings and the girl and all that spooky stuff back at the house – they're all connected, aren't they? Besides, you saw her first, remember? Wasn't she poking about the sketchbooks?'

I nodded. 'It was just a fleeting glance.'

'Well, you were able to describe her well enough to me,' retorted Susy. 'Fleeting glance or not, it's definitely the same girl … I wish I'd never bought those cruddy sketchbooks. All these weird things happening and now this – Mrs Powell getting bad – what have we let ourselves into, Arty?'

'I don't know,' I admitted. 'But, whatever it is, I don't think we've seen the end of it.'

5

When we got home, Susy disappeared, leaving me to answer Mum's questions. I didn't mention that the old lady had been talking about the Smythes when it happened. I probably would have been blamed and I didn't need that sort of hassle. Mum, of course, immediately swept over to the Home to see about Mrs Powell.

Dad was down in the shop, polishing some dingy lamps. I went to my room and wandered over to the window, trying not to think of Mrs Powell's gasping breath and all that heavy medical machinery. I took the sketch out of my pocket to have another look at it, to work out just why it was giving off such creepy vibes.

It was then, while I had my back to the room, that I got this chilling feeling, as if icy fingers were playing the xylophone along my spine. The same eerie feeling that I'd had when I was stuck in that dreary hall. I crumpled the sketch into my fist.

Then I felt it rustle like someone or something was trying to take it from me.

'That you, Susy?' My voice sounded flat

and unreal through my knuckles. There was no reply. I was being frozen into a terrified zombie by whatever was in the room behind me. Conscious of being watched, I tensed, waiting to be tapped on the shoulder.

'Arty!'

I fell against the window with fright. When my brain got the message that it was Susy's voice, I turned. Her face was as white as mine felt from the inside.

'It's her!' she went on, her voice shaking. 'She was in my room again. I'm not dreaming. She was for real. Come on.'

'Come on where?' I croaked.

'To my room.'

'Hell, no! I'm getting out of here.'

Susy grabbed my hand, then dropped it. 'It's freezing,' she said. 'Just like ...'

'Like when I was stuck in the door of that cruddy house,' I whispered. 'Didn't you feel the chill? When you saw that girl, did you feel it? A horrible chilling feeling?'

Susy shook her head. She shivered slightly. 'No, nothing like that in my room. In fact, I wasn't all that scared.'

'Come off it,' I said. 'All this spooky stuff and you say you weren't scared?'

'No, Arty,' Susy said. 'She's trying to tell us something. I'll show you.'

'No way. I'm not chasing after any spook,'

I insisted. 'Let's get out.'

Susy didn't budge. 'She needs help.'

'Are you nuts?' I said. 'She's a spook for heaven's sake! What's wrong with you?'

'I'm telling you,' Susy said urgently. 'I think there's something she wants us to do. Anyway she's gone, so you needn't worry; you won't see her. She was just there for a few seconds, same as before.'

'Susy!' I peered closely at my cousin to check for signs of spooky hypnosis or something. 'You're *standing* there calmly telling me you've just seen a ghost and you want to *help* her?'

'Yes. Come on with me.'

She half dragged me to her room. At the door I closed my eyes in case I'd be confronted by something I'd rather not see. This was like one of those nightmares that make you keep wanting to wake up but can't.

'Look at that,' said Susy. 'Open your eyes, you wally.'

I opened them one at a time so that I'd only have half a scare. The sketchbooks were scattered across the floor.

'I had tidied away all these after last night.' Susy pointed towards the sketchbooks. 'I was just dozing on my bed when she came, just now. She was looking at them. I was petrified. I tried to shout, but couldn't. She looked at me and – I know you don't believe this – but I didn't feel quite so scared. Not when I saw her face, especially her eyes. There was no harm in her eyes.'

'Susy,' I said. 'You must have been scared. This is a *spook* we're talking about here. I'd be a gabbling mess by now, if it was I who saw her. That's what normal people do if they see a ghost. I've read about these things. They go stark raving mad. And you're just talking as if ...'

Susy was shaking her head. 'She pointed to these,' she went on. 'And then she looked at me as if she was begging.'

'Yeah,' I snorted. 'Sure, Susy. Let's go.'

'Listen! She especially pointed to this page.' Susy picked up a loose drawing. It was another view of Heather Grange. 'Look, it has a sort of thumb mark on it. That wasn't there before. This drawing was sparkly clean last time I saw it, and nobody has touched it since.' She thrust it under my nose. 'I didn't touch that. Did you touch it?'

'No way,' I replied. But the mark was there, clear as day. And, like Susy, I knew it hadn't been there before. I'm very good at noticing details like that. I peered more closely at it. And then I realised something. I took the other sketch out of my pocket and smoothed it out.

'Wow!' said Susy. I'd have said 'wow' too, but the word stuck in my throat. We both looked at the two drawings. The thumb mark on the second drawing was right where the attic window used to be!

'That mark is covering the window,' said Susy. 'What does it mean?' she went on.

'Haven't a clue,' I said. 'But something weird is going on. Either that or you and I should be locked up. Do you think we're imagining things?' I hoped she'd laugh and say yes, of course we were. I didn't mention the scare I'd had before she'd burst on to the scene – partly from cowardice and partly because I wanted to believe it was just a sudden draught, that my nerves were on overdrive. Susy shook her head.

'It's a message,' she said. 'That girl is trying to tell us something, I'm sure of it.'

'Tell us what?'

'I don't know, but it's all to do with that attic window.'

I thrust the drawing with the thumb mark into Susy's hands – it had been touched by a ghost. I put the other one back in my pocket.

'Look,' I said. 'Let's go downstairs and tell Dad about this. He'll know what to do.'

'Your da? He'll laugh like a maniac and tell us we're a couple of nerds,' muttered Susy.

True. Dad had little time for hocus-pocus. He scoffed at Mum's attempts at Feng-Shui and burning oils, saying that stuff belonged to the days of wizards and weirdos.

'What then?' I spluttered. 'Do we just hang around and wait for more spooky stuff? Maybe next time she'll bring a couple of pals and we can have a party.'

'Well, have you a better idea, cleverclogs?'

Of course I hadn't. I just wished that Mum or Dad would rush in and tell us to get packed, that we were going on a surprise holiday. As if. We went downstairs and offered to help Dad polish some of his lamps. Well, Susy did, but I got roped in as well. At least it was comforting sitting in the shop doing something ordinary and watching the passers-by doing normal things like going to the video store across the street or carrying brown bags from the Chinese take-away. Now and then I glanced questioningly at Susy, tempted to spill the beans to Dad, but she just frowned and shook her head.

I dreaded the night ahead. So I finally decided it was time to see if Dad might be receptive towards matters spooky. Avoiding Susy's eyes I turned towards Dad.

'Dad,' I said, trying to sound carefree and normal. 'Do you believe in ghosts?'

Dad gave me a look and began to chortle.

'Of course I do,' he replied. That wasn't the logical, calming answer I was looking for. My heart sank. Then he added, 'There's a whole bunch of them working in the Inland Revenue – tax office to you and me. They're the ones that lurk around every business deal so that they can get their scary hairy paws on your few sweat-earned shekels. Ghosts? Ha! Shower of faceless creeps. A wooden stake through the heart is too good for them!'

'No, Dad, I'm serious. Do you believe in *real* ghosts?'

'You mean spectres in shrouds, or guys carrying their lopped-off heads under their arms? Not in a million years. Dead is dead. Hole in the ground. End of story. Rest in peace, amen. Why do you ask? Some spook hop out of your wardrobe and say boo?'

'Just wondering.' Any thoughts of support from my father went right out of my head. It wouldn't be worth the blast of teasing we'd get if we tried to tell him of recent events. I glanced guiltily at Susy and she gave me a triumphant 'told-you-so' glare.

'What about Mum?' I went on, clutching at straws. 'Does she believe in ghosts?'

Dad laughed again. 'Your mum might be a bit of an earth mother,' he said, 'with her daft holistic hoo-ha and her fancy oils, but that's as far as it goes – the earth. Her beliefs are firmly stuck here on the planet we live on. Hope you're not going weird on us,' he added, looking at me.

'Ha!' I said. Feeble response, I know. But I was in a feeble condition.

Later on Mum came back. She'd seen the light in the shop so she came in by the shop door. She looked at Susy and me with surprise. If she'd said anything about me working I'd have said something very rude because of the throbbing through my head. But she didn't. Instead she talked about Mrs Powell.

'Poor dear,' she said. 'She's just lying there like a bag of bones. Such lovely, delicate features. She must have been a beauty.'

'Mum,' I said, 'you're not saying she's ... she's dead, are you?'

Mum shook her head. 'No. She sometimes gets these mild black-outs. But she'll be fine. As if she hadn't enough to contend with.'

'What do you mean?' asked Dad.

Mum grimaced. 'She told me recently that she doesn't know if she can afford to stay much longer at the Home. It's very expensive. She doesn't know where she'll go if she has to leave. She loves it there.'

I breathed a sigh of relief. At least I wouldn't have her death on my conscience, as well as all the other mind-boggling stuff.

'Why couldn't she have waited until after her conversation with me to have her bad turn?' I muttered to Susy. 'Long enough to tell us about that cruddy house and its spooky past.'

Susy flicked me with her polishing cloth. 'Selfish prat,' she said. 'That's all you can think about? If you hadn't given the poor thing the third degree, she'd be fine.'

'Ah, so it's my fault, is it? I knew it would come back to me. And can you explain, Miss Knowall, why our lives are sinking into some spooky, grabby quicksand because of stupid drawings that you should have left alone?'

Susy breathed on her lamp and polished it vigorously. 'Buzz off,' she said eventually.

To buzz off like a carefree bee, with nothing to worry about except the where-abouts of the next smelly flower, would have been the ultimate happiness just then. I'd have settled to be anything rather than the nervous wreck I was fast becoming.

6

I left my bedroom door open all night, just to
have a quick exit in case of trouble. But there
wasn't any. Trouble I mean. No white faces
– neither Susy's nor the scary one – loomed
in the night. It was good to wake up with the
sun driving away all eerie thoughts.

'What are you two planning today?' asked
Mum at breakfast.

I looked at Susy. 'Swimming. We're going
to the pool. Then to …'

'To the library,' put in Susy.

'The library?' Mum looked at me with
disbelief. I concentrated on my Weetabix.
Susy and her bright ideas! As if Mum would
believe I'd go to the library unless she was
hauling me along.

'Yes,' said Susy. 'We're going to look up
some local history, isn't that right, Arty?'

I concentrated even more on my bowl.

'Local history?' said Mum. 'Are you still
thinking about that house in the sketchbooks? Heather Grange?'

Susy beamed at Mum. 'We are, Una,' she
said, all smooth charm. 'It's a fascinating old
place, isn't it?'

I spluttered, the milk going up my nose. More than anything I wanted to tell Mum, now that she'd brought up the subject of the old house again. But I got a warning look from Susy – always one step ahead of me.

'Can you remember anything more about it?' Susy went on.

Mum shook her head. 'Not really.'

'Anything at all?' Susy projected curious innocence.

'Way before my time,' said Mum. 'But there was something about a young daughter. Marie or Maria, I think she was called. Only child. Wealthy parents. I seem to remember that the parents died tragically – an accident I think.'

'What happened the girl?' asked Susy, picking the raisins out of Mum's homemade muesli.

Mum shook her head again. 'Some uncle came to look after her and run the estate. But that's as much as I know.'

'His name,' persisted Susy. 'Can you remember his name?'

Mum laughed. 'You really are stuck on this old place, aren't you, Susy?'

'Just interested. I own the pictures of it so I'd like to know as much as possible.'

'Una,' Dad called from the foot of the stairs. 'Shop busy.'

Mum got up and went over to the mirror.

'You two be okay?' she said.

'Don't worry about us,' said Susy. 'We'll have fun.'

The way she said it and the way she looked at me set off alarms inside my head.

'James,' said Mum as she went through the door.

'What?' Susy and I said together.

'The uncle. His name was James. I remember my mother mentioned it once. He came to look after the place. Must dash. Cheerio.'

Susy looked at me triumphantly. 'See?' she said. 'It's all piecing together.'

'What's all piecing together?'

'Everything,' she went on. 'Mrs Powell said something about "that James", remember? As if it left a bad taste in her mouth.'

'Could be coincidence,' I said.

'I don't believe that,' said Susy. 'I just wish I knew what happened.' She clattered the dishes she was gathering to express her frustration. 'What happened the parents and what happened when that James bloke took over? Do you think did he bump off the parents and then the girl to get his hands on the estate?'

'You're stuck into a fantasy, Susy,' I said. 'Get real. He probably just sold the place and took the kid with him. End of story.'

Susy was shaking her head. 'So, if they sold out, why didn't the new owners move in? Why has the house been idle all these years?'

'That's easy,' I forced a laugh. 'Whoever bought the land didn't want the house. It happens all the time. Ask my da. He knows all about property from going around to house auctions. People who already have a family home but want to add to their land will buy up another farm and just let the house on that land fall into ruin.'

'Even a big house like Heather Grange? Don't be daft. Anyone who'd buy a place like that would want to live in it.'

'Maybe not. Big old houses like that cost money to keep. It's cheaper to let them go to ruin.'

Susy gave a sharp sniff which told me how highly she thought of my reasoning.

'Look,' I said. 'Could we just get out of here? My nerves are jittery. I can't believe we're having an ordinary conversation after what's been going on. We should be jabbering wrecks.'

'Speak for yourself,' retorted Susy.

It wasn't the usual, cheerful librarian. It was a thin-faced wrinkly who had anti-kids written all over him – obviously someone who'd been dusted up and taken from a shelf to fill in for the regular librarian who was on holidays. He gritted his plastic teeth when we asked for access to the computer to surf through back-dated local newspapers.

'Hope you two aren't just coming in to mess about,' he said. 'Sunny day like this. Your lot come in here, chew gum and make a nuisance of yourselves.'

'Our lot!' exclaimed Susy. 'Listen ...'

'History project,' I interrupted quickly, before Susy could get worked up. 'Local research.'

The man led us to the line of computers and set us up. 'No gum,' he said.

'Haven't you?' said Susy sweetly. 'You can have some of mine.'

That brought us a threatening glower.

'Prat,' hissed Susy after the librarian's retreating back. 'I've a good mind to ...'

'To do nothing and shut up,' I said. 'Let's get this out of the way. Where will we start?'

'Try the late nineteen thirties,' said Susy. 'That was your granny's time.'

And so we did. Until our eyes were tickled dizzy by the flashing print. But nothing turned up about Heather Grange or people called Smythe. After half an hour we were stuck into the beginnings of World War Two.

I yawned and stretched myself. 'I'm sick of

this,' I said. 'There's nothing. We're wasting our time.'

'We can't give up yet,' said Susy. 'Let's go back to the early thirties.'

'Why?'

She shrugged. 'Just a hunch.'

'You and your hunches,' I scoffed. Still, I did as she said and we scanned through 1930 and 1931. Then, in June 1932, we hit the jackpot. Front page headlines!

'There it is!' exclaimed Susy, so loudly that I thought we'd be thrown out.

'TRAGIC ACCIDENT IN ENGLAND' went the heading. Susy and I put our heads together and read on:

A tragic accident has claimed the lives of two of Cashelderry's most respected and distinguished people. While motoring to Holyhead to catch the ferry to Kingstown, Mr Alfred Smythe and his beautiful wife, Alice, were killed when their motor car hit a tree on a sharp incline in the Welsh hills. It is thought that their motor went out of control. Both of them were killed instantly.

The whole village of Cashelderry is devastated by this dreadful news. The couple had been holidaying with Mr James Smythe in England. Mr and Mrs Smythe resided at Heather Grange, home to the Smythe family for over two centuries. During the famine of 1846, Heather

Grange offered sustenance to the peasantry for miles around, saving countless lives. For several generations the estate has given employment to many of the local villagers who worked on the land, the stud farm and in the mansion. Condolences are offered to James and to dear little Maria, daughter of the deceased. Mrs Smythe, formerly from France, was an only child whose parents died several years ago. Funeral arrangements will be announced at a later date.

'Car went out of control,' Susy said.

'It can happen,' I said. 'Especially old bangers like they had back then.'

'I don't believe it,' said Susy.

'Oh, Susy,' I exclaimed. 'It's here in black and white.'

She shook her head. 'Something smells not right,' she went on. 'Just a hunch.'

'Not another one of your daft ones!'

She took a notebook out of the small rucksack she'd brought and wrote down the details in the article. Then we clicked ahead to the funeral which took place a week later. Full page coverage about people being sorely missed, wonderful family, sad, dreary, lots of woe, Cashelderry would never be the same … all the usual stuff that's always said at funerals. Then a list of mourners.

'There was a cousin,' said Susy, several lines ahead of me. 'See?' she pointed to the screen:

Little Maria, now a tragic orphan, was accompanied by her mother's French cousin, Janetta, who comforted the child throughout the sad ceremony.

'French cousin,' Susy said. I could see that her mind was ticking. 'I wonder.'

'Wonder what?' I knew I'd probably regret asking.

'I bet there was something going on between the French cousin and that James,' she went on. 'They dumped the kid and took everything.'

'Come off it, Susy,' I protested.

'Think about it,' she said. 'The girl in the blue dress has to be Maria.'

'So why is she spooking us?' I asked. 'What are we supposed to do?'

'It's the attic!' whispered Susy. 'She put that thumb mark on the place where the attic window was. I wish I knew why. Maybe her body is in there.'

I began to speak, but Susy shushed me.

'I see it now,' she said. 'They killed Maria and put her body in the attic. We have to find out what happened. Bet we'd find her body in the attic.'

'No!' I said. 'What good would that do? You some kind of masochist or something, wanting to scare yourself – and me – into mental cases? Or even an early death?'

'Well, we have to do something,' muttered Susy. 'I couldn't stand that, never knowing when Maria Smythe is going to visit me with her pleading eyes. I bet she wants us to find her body.'

I took a deep breath that came out very shakily. Even my lungs were nervous.

'Look. We'll ask Mrs Powell,' I said. 'She's our last hope. She'll tell us what to do.'

'Mrs Powell?' Susy looked aghast. 'She's sick. Have you forgotten yesterday?'

'She's not too bad,' I said. 'Mum said so. She has these turns all the time, but she bounces back. It's an old-person thing.'

Susy shrugged. 'Okay,' she said.

7

'You two are a pretty responsible pair, aren't you?' Dad asked at lunch. 'You and Susy?'

I wondered where this was leading.

'Well able to look after yourselves?'

'Why are you asking all this?' said Susy, cutting to the core as usual.

Dad shuffled a bit and glanced at Mum. 'It's this auction ...' he began.

'Oh no!' I put in. 'Not an auction. Dad, I'd rather take a dip with a bunch of friendly piranhas. Auctions are out.'

'Not you,' said Dad. 'Your Mum and me. There's a big house auction over in Galway tomorrow – Gowan House – and it coincides with our closing day. We thought we'd go along this evening and stay the night so that we'd be able to view before the auction starts. How about it?'

'How about what?' I asked.

'Would you two be all right here on your own?' put in Mum. 'Just until tomorrow evening. If not you could come along.'

'And be bored mindless. Thanks,' I said.

'Are you sure?' continued Mum. I could see that she and Dad were straining at the leash to get away, probably have some posh nosh in a fancy hotel before buying in another load of dusty junk for us all to polish.

'Of course we'll be okay, Una,' smiled Susy. It was only then I realised that Susy and I would be on our own.

'If we did go …' I began.

'We're not going,' Susy cut in. 'Stop trying to complicate things. We'll be grand here. You go ahead,' she said to my parents. 'Just as long as there's plenty of grub.'

Mum needn't have looked so relieved. She could at least have shown some regret at leaving her only son to a chilling fate.

'There's a ghost in the house.' I couldn't hold back. 'A dead girl who's haunting us.'

Dead silence. Then Dad burst out laughing. 'Back to spooks? Thought we'd covered that. Offer her some bangers and mash, then send her back to Never-Never Land.'

'Arty!' said Mum. 'What are you playing at? One minute you say you'd be bored to death at an auction, the next minute you're throwing up ghosts so that you can come with us. Come if you like. There's no need for bizarre excuses.'

'Don't mind him, Una,' said Susy. 'The lad's mad, you should know that by now.' She turned and gave me a scathing look.

'Well, if you're sure. There are pizzas in

the freezer and lots of ice cream.'

Dad threw a fiver on the table. 'Get yourselves a video,' he said. 'No scary stuff,' he added, looking meaningfully at me. 'Stick to Walt Disney, but no Blair Witches or any of that nonsense.'

I tried to say 'Huh' but it died on me.

'How is Mrs Powell?' Susy asked Mum, nicely changing the subject.

'She's fine,' Mum replied. 'It was just a mild black-out. She's been moved to a ward, but she's sitting up and in fairly good form. Says she's tormented by nightmares, poor thing. Wakes up sweating and weak.'

'Well, nobody ever died of nightmares,' said Dad. 'We all have those.'

'Would she like us to visit?' asked Susy in her put-on angelic voice.

'What a nice thought, Susy,' said Mum. 'But I don't know. She's still very weak...'

'We'll just pat her hand,' I put in. 'Just to show that we're thinking of her. After all, we were there when it happened.'

Mum's eyebrows shot up. 'That's very noble of you, Arty,' she said. 'I didn't think you were into sick-bed visits.'

'No need for sarcasm, Mum,' I said brusquely. 'I'm just trying to do a good turn for an old lady. Do you have to put the mockers on?'

Mum stretched out her hand and smiled apologetically. 'Sorry, honeybun,' she said. 'Of course go up and see her if you want to. But bear in mind that she's pretty weak and she won't be able for any banter. Just hold her hand and make soothing noises ...'

'Mum! Don't go overboard. We just want to see how she is.'

Mum sighed. 'Okay. Just bear in mind that they might not let you in without an adult.'

'What ward is she in?' I asked.

'Saint Joseph's,' Mum replied. There was a doubt in her voice. 'Don't bet on getting in. They get over-fussy in cases like hers.'

'We'll get in,' I said with determination. We had to get to see Mrs Powell. Our sanity, maybe our lives, depended on what the old lady could tell us.

I hung around for as long as possible, willing my parents to change their minds about going. At the same time I didn't want to appear to be a total wimp, both in their eyes and, above all, in Susy's. How she was being so calm I couldn't fathom. You'd think everything was normal from the way she was going on. Maybe she really was mad. Maybe we both were – some genetic thing that breaks out every few years.

'You two sure you'll be all right on your own?' said Mum, turning back at the door.

No, I wanted to scream, *take us with you!*

'We'll be fine,' Susy laughed. 'Off you go and have a good time.'

We paused outside the hospital wing of the Home. I kept watch while Susy nicked some more flowers.

'What if they won't let us into the ward?' I said. 'It's different from just visiting Mrs Powell in her own room.'

Susy frowned. 'Always the one with the negative vibes, aren't you, Arty?'

'Vibes me eye!' I muttered. 'If we don't find out more about that old house, we could have that dead kid around our necks for the rest of our lives, like that guy who shot the albatross.'

'Someone shot an albatross?' exclaimed Susy, getting her priorities foggy as usual.

'It's a poem,' I said. ' "The Ancient Mariner".' Dad had read it to me when I was eight, but it sounds better when you let on that you've actually read it yourself.

'Oh, only a poem,' Susy scoffed. 'I didn't know you were into poetry.'

'Let's just get on with this,' I said. 'We've got to think of a way to get in without the heavies saying we should be with an adult.'

As if in answer to that, a car pulled up at the entrance and a mumsy-looking woman got out. Quick as a flash Susy dragged me up the steps and opened the door for her. She smiled graciously at us.

'Saint Teresa's?' the woman said, looking questioningly at the receptionist.

'Next left, third door,' was the reply.

The receptionist didn't even give Susy and me a second glance as we stuck close to the stout lady's heels. Plan A completed. Now to find Saint Joseph's. Why did wards have to be called after saints, I wondered as I looked up at the signposts which pointed in the direction of the various wards?

'Can I help you?' A tall nurse in a blue uniform was looking suspiciously at Susy and me and the bunch of flowers that were fast going limp. 'Are you with somebody?'

I paused to get my reflexes together.

'Yes. Our mother,' Susy said, pointing vaguely after the lady on whose coat-tails we'd come in. 'Saint Joseph's...'

'Second corridor on the right,' said the nurse. 'Stay with your mother and don't be wandering around on your own.' She bustled off to torture some bedridden victim.

'Quick,' I hissed. 'Let's find Mrs Powell before we're found out.'

8

We found Mrs Powell's ward, no problem. Maybe it had something to do with the picture outside of a man in a brown dress clutching a carpenter's hammer, his tragic eyes looking up at a heaven beyond the peeling ceiling. Thankfully Mrs Powell was on her own – no other old ladies to earwig our conversation. Her eyelids flickered for a moment and then she looked straight at me with the familiar directness that always made me feel I was special. She smiled. 'Arty,' she whispered, closing her eyes again.

'And me, Susy,' said my feisty cousin, muscling in front of me.

A nurse passed by the open door, pushing a trolley filled with bottles and phials.

'Here comes the drug-pusher,' Susy whispered into Mrs Powell's ear. 'You want a fix?'

Mrs Powell smiled slightly. It was okay, she could still respond to a bit of fun. That was a relief. The nurse looked at Susy and me.

'Are you relations?' she asked.

'Of course,' I replied. That was no lie; Susy and I were definitely related.

Mrs Powell came to the rescue. She

opened her eyes and raised her hand.

'Leave them,' she said, in a tired whisper.

The nurse shrugged again before moving along to shove some disgusting-looking concoctions down the throats of her charges.

'Mrs Powell,' I moved my chair nearer to her head and leaned closer, 'are you all right? Would you like us to leave?'

She smiled and pressed my hand.

'Glad to see you both,' she began. She closed her eyes and nodded again. Good sense told me that it wouldn't do to start questioning her about the Smythe place. Not yet. I told her about the shop and Man United. Susy told her what was happening in 'Coronation Street' and 'Fair City'. Then I came to the point.

'You remember that old sketch I showed you?' I began. 'Of Heather Grange?'

Her eyes shot open and she looked at me intently. I felt the bony pressure of her fingers dig into my hand.

'Arty,' she whispered. 'Leave it alone.'

'I have to know,' I whispered back. 'We've been there, Mrs Powell. There's something there. Something that has... has followed us. I'm scared. You must tell me. People say that something bad happened there long ago. Did something bad happen? Please! We need your help.'

She painfully turned her head so that she was looking at me face on. I recoiled when I saw her expression. It seemed like she wanted to say a lot, but the words were trapped inside her sick body. 'Arty,' she said again. 'Oh, Arty! I'm so sorry. There's no turning back now. He knows. Oh, he knows.'

I leaned over to catch any whisper.

'Go on, ' I encouraged her. 'Who knows what? There *is* something, isn't there? You know what happened? It's to do with the drawing, isn't it?'

'Cool it, Arty,' said Susy. 'Maybe this is too upsetting.

'Back again,' Mrs Powell breathed. 'You must... He won't stop until... '

She eased herself back on to her pillow. We waited for her to say something else, but she stayed quiet.

'She's asleep,' whispered Susy. 'Her face is all twisted, like there's a lot going on inside her head. We've got to leave her alone.'

I knew we should. But I was clinging to straws and she was the only one we had.

'Who or what's back?' I asked, ignoring Susy's tug at my arm. 'Please, Mrs Powell.'

I hadn't noticed the nurse abandoning her trolley until I felt the tap on my shoulder.

'Right, sunshine,' she said. 'Time to go. You're upsetting Mrs Powell. I knew you shouldn't have been let up here. Now, off you go, there's a good lad. Follow your sister's example and let the woman rest.'

Susy waved to me from the door. The rotten creep, she was scarpering.

'Mrs Powell,' I began desperately, seeing my last hope for help fade away. 'Please...'

'Out!' commanded the nurse, propelling me round by the arm. I looked at her pleadingly. 'Out!' she said again. I glanced back at Mrs Powell in the hope that she might put in a word for me, but something had stirred up troubled memories. Then, for a second, the eyelids flicked open again. I could see she was fighting to speak.

I pulled away from the pincer-grip on my shoulder and bent over Mrs Powell's bed.

'You must,' she gasped. 'You must... he won't stop until you find... chest.'

'What?' I cried, as once more I was roughly pulled away.

Mrs Powell uttered a single word again. 'Chest.'

'Let her finish what she's trying to tell me,' I said angrily.

'You callous little brat,' said the nurse, pushing me ahead of her. 'She's saying she has a pain in her chest. The poor dear. You kids never stop to think that someone might be suffering. How dare you come in here and upset her. Out before I call security.'

'Cow!' I muttered as I rubbed my arm, trying to keep down the panic of seeing any answer to this mess disappear.

'Thanks for running off like that,' I said to Susy when I caught up with her at the gate. 'You could have stayed to back me up.'

'No way,' she said. 'That poor woman had had enough of our company. I wasn't going to hang around to make her miserable. I could see there was no point. We shouldn't have come. Why couldn't you see that?'

I kicked at a stone, forgetting I was wearing light runners. The pain prevented me from arguing as I bit my lip to stop crying out. I knew I shouldn't have gone on questioning Mrs Powell. No matter how I tried to justify it to myself, I couldn't chase away the image of her pained expression.

'Did she say anything?' Susy went on.

'If you'd stayed for a few seconds longer you'd have heard for yourself,' I said miffily.

'Oh, stop being such a baby. What did she say? Exact words. No added-in bits.'

I put my hands in my pockets and hunched my shoulders miserably. Bad enough to have my conscience nagging, but the fact that there was little or nothing to show for it made me feel even worse.

'She was just rambling,' I said.

'Rambling? How rambling?'

'About someone coming back.'

'I heard that part,' said Susy. 'Maybe she meant you, that you'd come back to see her. That makes sense.'

I shrugged. 'Maybe. Then she said – what was it? "He won't stop until you find..." Then after a pause she said, "chest".'

'Chest?'

'Yes. The nurse said she must have been having a pain in her chest.'

Susy was frowning. She said nothing, but I knew she was twisting and turning those few words around in her head.

'Like I said,' I went on, not liking the silence. 'She was just rambling.'

'I don't think so,' said Susy. 'She wasn't rambling. She was upset when you mentioned the house. If she'd been rambling she wouldn't have really heard what you said. She heard all right, and she was trying to tell you something.'

'Huh, none of it makes sense,' I said. 'And who's the "he" who won't stop until we find it – whatever *it* is?'

We were to find that out sooner than we expected.

9

My parents had left by the time we got home. The house seemed extra quiet and gloomy. I told myself that it was my nerves on overdrive, but it didn't help.

'Wish we'd gone with them,' I said.

'I don't,' said Susy. 'We're stuck in the middle of some mystery that only we can work out, and we can't ignore it.'

'Why just us?' I asked. 'Why can't we tell someone?'

'Tell who?' asked Susy, busily rooting out pizzas from the freezer. 'You saw how your folks reacted to your ghost bit. Do you want us to scream it on the street? That would bring a reaction all right – like men in white coats and a wagon to take us to the nearest funny-farm. Light the oven and let's get these pizzas on, I'm starving.'

Later on we picked up a couple of videos from across the street. Comedies. I insisted on comedies. It was getting dark by the time we returned. Dark always brings its own luggage of eeriness, but tonight it was dragging crates of the stuff.

I wished now, more than ever, that my

parents weren't away, that I could rub out the past couple of days. Wish, wish. what a useless word. Here was the night falling, with all its pending dread, and there was nothing I could do about it.

We stayed watching the videos until around twelve-thirty. Susy yawned and stretched herself.

'I'm for bed,' she said, striking a chord of panic in me.

'You're not heading off alone?' I said.

She shrugged. 'Nothing will happen. I'm telling you, there's something about that girl that's sort of warm and alive. She's not like a spook, even though we only get flashes of her.'

I couldn't understand her calmness, until I thought back to the time I'd seen the girl in the blue dress at the auction. Susy was right; she did seem harmless. But why had I got the same icy vibes that time I'd been looking at the sketch as I'd got in the old house? Something didn't balance out.

While Susy was brushing her fangs in the bathroom, I pulled the camp-bed from the spare room into hers.

'What do you think you're doing?' Susy looked at me with disbelief when she came back.

'Thought you'd like company,' I said,

rolling up my jeans and tucking them under my pillow for extra support.

Susy gave a horrible cackle. 'You want the company, you wally,' she said. 'Who are you kidding? You're scared out of your tiny mind. I keep telling you, Arty, this girl doesn't scare me. She's not out to harm us. You don't harm people you need, and she seems to need us.'

'And we need her like a hole in the head,' I retorted. I must have looked every bit the scared wreck I was because she looked at me with scorn.

'Okay, you can crash down there for the night,' she said. 'But one snore or one silly nightmare muttering and you're out of here, okay?'

I nodded. I was fuming that she was lording it over me, but I pressed my lips together. I didn't want her to dump me out on my ear. I read for a while, but the words were just shapes on paper. Waste of time. I turned out the lamp to try to get some sleep. The sudden dark didn't feel ominous because I could hear Susy's even breathing. A comforting sound. I sighed and turned over. But sleep didn't come.

It was around two o'clock that the first chilling thing happened. When I heard the rustle I froze, fighting to cancel out the frightening images my brain was throwing up. But when the now-familiar chill crept over me, I knew that a whole scary scene was about to unfold. Damp. Decay. The musty smell you get in the greengrocer's on a Saturday evening when unsold veggies begin to go off. I braced myself. My hands flew instinctively to protect my head. Why did this unseen thing hate me? Why me, of all the people in the world?

I began to flay about in panic.

'Get off!' I shouted, with all the anger I could scrape together.

That woke Susy.

'What are you at, Arty?'

'It's happening, Susy,' I cried shakily. 'It's all happening.'

'Take it easy,' she said, her voice only slightly comforting in the dark. 'I knew you'd get stuck into some nightmare. I hear nothing. Turn on the light.'

I warily stretched my hand out. Click. Nothing happened. Click. Click. Click.

'Dead,' I cried. 'The light's dead!'

'It's just that the bulb is gone. Cheapo bulbs. Get your folks to buy quality...'

'Shut up!' I screamed.

Susy broke off as the cold vibes reached her. Nothing to see, nothing to hear, just a feeling so intense that I could hear my own brain slushing inside my head. With a bound Susy landed beside me and we both cowered, waiting for a physical attack. We clung to one another, too petrified to cry out.

Again and again the chilling presence advanced and retreated in a macabre dance.

'Stop!' I managed to cry out at last. 'Get away, you cowardly creep!'

Fat lot of good that did. Even with the duvet pulled over our heads, the chilling presence was everywhere. We were suffocating and freezing at the same time.

'What is it?' gasped Susy. 'What the hell is it?'

Again and again it chilled its way into our bones.

Then there was a different sound.

'Books,' I whispered. 'Sounds like books being thrown around.'

It came from the spare room next door.

The clunk of falling books and the rustle of papers were now the only sounds to break the night. Susy eased her head above the duvet.

'See anything?' I asked.

'Nothing.'

I peered over the duvet myself. Pitch black. In a way I was glad that this room was at the back of the house, away from the glow of the street lights. But when the damp stench began to come towards us again, I wanted to see it, face on. Whatever evil, ugly thing it was, I wanted to shout at it and beat it with my fists. Fear had turned to anger – scared anger.

'Quick!' gasped Susy.

'Quick what?'

'Let's get the hell out of here,' She grabbed my arm and pulled me out of my zombie state. We dashed through the oppressive darkness to the open door.

We burst out on to the landing, felt for the banisters and clattered down the stairs towards the front door. As I reached up for the catch, the musty presence surrounded us, making us gag. And this time we felt it. With ghostly force it threw us against the door, stopping both of us from reaching the catch. Each time we tried to move, it forced us back. Together we sank into a huddle on the floor, shielding our faces against the onslaught.

Like before, the unseen thing advanced and retreated, each advance wrapping us in an overwhelming aura that seemed to suck us into a vortex of black nothingness. Was this really happening in my own house? Were we just the thickness of a door away from a world where we could get help?

When I thought I heard Susy cry out I raised my head. But it wasn't Susy who'd cried out. At the top of the stairs I saw a flash of blue, a lacy dress. The image was so fleeting it was almost subliminal, but it was long enough for me to recognise the girl in blue. The cold stench suddenly left Susy and me and seemed to hurl itself towards that flutter of blue. I blinked. Then both the blue and the icy chill were gone.

It was all over so quickly that I wondered if this whole business was just happening inside my head. When Susy spoke it brought me back to reality.

'Gone,' she whispered. 'It's gone.'

'Did you see her?'

'Was it her?' Susy asked. 'It was so quick...'

'Of course it was her,' I said. 'Blue dress.'

'That...that thing, it chased after her,' whispered Susy. 'She saved us from that thing by drawing it away from us.'

I nodded, and swallowed really hard. 'It was as if it was trying to get her,' I said.

'Why?' asked Susy. 'There's something pretty stinky going on here, Arty. It looks like there are two ghosts.'

'You see? I was right,' I said. 'There *was* something that followed us back from that cruddy house. Something that has it in for us.' I reached up and opened the front door.

'What are you doing?' asked Susy, as the

fresh night air washed over us.

'I'm going next door,' I replied.

'And tell them what?' Susy went on. 'That we've been chased by one ghost and saved by another? Yeah, sure, Arty. They'll really believe a story like that.'

'I'm not staying here,' I said, still holding the door open. By the street light I could see Susy's white face. I knew she was right. Murphys next door would hardly roll out the red carpet if Susy and I came hammering at their door at half-past two in the morning with a tale of things going bump.

'It's over,' she said. 'Can't you feel it? And look, the lights are working.'

She'd reached up and switched on the hall light. I looked fearfully up at the landing, but it looked normal.

'What should we do then?' I asked, reluctantly closing the door.

'We'll go back upstairs and see what damage that stupid eejit did.'

I knew her brave talk was hiding her fear. I wished I could do the same. Apart from running screaming down the street, we hadn't any choice but to gather the shreds of our sanity and hold the hysterics at bay. We turned on every light switch between the hall and the spare room. At the door we paused.

'You first,' I said to Susy.

'Yeah, right,' she snorted.

As we ventured in together, Susy gave a low whistle.

'Look at that mess,' she said.

Books were scattered all over the floor, as if a tornado had whisked them up and thrown them around. Dad's books and papers – this bedroom doubled as his office. He kept all his reference books in here. However, I was too scared of what was going on right now to consider his anger.

'Your dad will kill us,' said Susy.

'Yeah, well I'd prefer to be killed by my old man than by whatever did this,' I said. 'Come on, we'd better try and tidy them up. I wonder what it was looking for.'

'The going rate for antiques,' quipped Susy, holding up a book about valuing antiques. 'Maybe it has a neat stash of coffin handles it wants to offload for a few quid.'

'How can you make stupid jokes at a time like this?' I said.

'Because it's better than letting a thing like that turn us into jibbering idiots,' she replied. She was right, of course. But my sense of humour had been bypassed by my sense of survival.

We gathered up the books and put them back on the shelves.

When we went back to Susy's room she let out a cry.

'The sketchbooks!' she said. 'Look!'

I turned nervously to where she was pointing, afraid of what I might see. But there were no wraiths or homicidal hellhounds. The sketchbooks, cause of all our trouble, were lying under the shelf where Susy had put them earlier. They were ripped apart, the torn pages strewn about like big confetti. That's when Susy's bravado gave out. She dashed across the room and began to gather the bits of paper.

'This doesn't make any sense,' she whimpered. 'The malicious prat. There was no need for this.' Tears of frustration dripped down her nose.

'None of it makes sense, Susy,' I said. 'Let's just hope that creep got what it wanted and won't bother us again. Look, some pages are still okay.' I picked up the hard covers and looked inside.

'But this drawing of the house,' said Susy, looking at some tattered scraps. 'That thing has torn up the picture of the house.'

'I have the other one,' I said. 'A bit tatty, but at least it's in one piece.'

It was then it dawned on me; it was in the pocket of my jeans which were rolled up under my pillow. That thing was still after that drawing, and we'd been sitting on it!

A few sketches still remained. I gathered up torn pieces that we might be able to put together with sellotape.

It was when I picked up the second sketchbook that I noticed a difference.

'Something weird here,' I mumbled.

'No more weird stuff, thank you,' said Susy.

'No, look,' I explained, holding out the hard cover. 'See? This back cover is thicker than the front.'

Susy leaned over to look. She ran her hand over the endpapers on the front and then on the back. Then she picked at a corner of the back cover and pulled. We held our breath as the endpaper came away.

'Something sealed in here,' whispered Susy. We looked at one another, wondering would this draw more ghouls on us.

'Go on,' I said. 'We've come this far.'

A few more gentle pulls and the hidden object was revealed.

'A diary,' gasped Susy. 'It's a diary!'

10

'We're into something heavy here,' I said. Well, of course we were. Heavy just about described everything that had gone on so far. And now this. I dropped the diary like a hot potato.

'Arty!' said Susy.

'Sorry. Jeez, what do we do now?'

'We can read the bloomin' thing,' she said, picking up the loose pages. 'Come on. We'll go down to the kitchen. The Aga will be warmer than shivering with cold and fright up here.'

The kitchen was warm and, spooky happenings apart, comforting. At least we were downstairs and near the back door in case of more weird visitors, although Susy was adamant that the girl in the blue dress had banished the chilling creep. I wasn't so sure, but I put on a brave front.

Susy smoothed out the pages on the table and began to read to herself.

'Well, go on then, read out loud,' I said. 'I'm here too you know.'

'*August 17th 1932,*' she began. '*I'm writing this on my last night here in my own room.*

Janetta and I have decided that after what's happened we must leave immediately. She says that it is better that the three of us disappear together, that way nobody can pinpoint what really happened. I hate the thought of carrying this secret around with me for the rest of my life, but the alternative would mean so much trouble for Jake and his family.'

'Trouble?'

'Sshh, will you let me read it?' she said, turning the page.

'Mama used to say James was a ne'er-do-well. But to me he was a romantic figure. He was many years older than my father. He had been in the army and all over the world. I wished he would come back so that I could show him off to my friends.

'How I wish now that he'd never come that Easter. My father was delighted when the letter came to say that he was paying us a visit. Papa said they could put the past behind them. Mama had looked angry and shooed me from the room.

'Uncle James was everything I had dreamed he'd be – tall, handsome, fun. Papa showed him around the estate with pride. Although Mama stayed cool and civil I could see that she did not like him. I used to hear her say to Janetta, her cousin who had come to live with us when I was five, how she wished he'd go away. But to me uncle James was a hero. We rode out together.

'Before he left, James invited Mama and Papa to visit him in London. Mama declined, but Papa said yes. I was disgusted that I was not to be part of this trip because it was during school time. James said not to worry, that we'd be seeing much more of each other. Little did I realise how true that would be.

'Mama put a spray of rhododendrons in my room on the morning she left for London. It was very early and I was still in bed. She said that by the time those blossoms would begin to wilt she and Papa would be back. Those were the last words she spoke to me.'

'This is too sad,' said Susy. 'Here, Arty, you take over. Leave out the sad bits.'

I took the pages from her and read:

'When the news came that my parents had been killed, my world fell apart.'

'I said to leave out the sad bits,' put in Susy. 'Just skim over her words.'

'Okay.' I glanced down the page. 'James had lent them his car. They were to drive to Holyhead. They were to garage the car there, for James to collect later, and take the ferry home. But the car spun off the road at a sharp bend and crashed into a wall.' I stopped.

'Well?' said Susy expectantly.

'You said to leave out the sad bits.'

'I mean her words,' retorted Susy.

'The parents were killed ... listen.'

'*Janetta was great. She nursed me through my grief and managed the estate. We were beginning to get back on course again when James announced, about a year later, that he was coming home. At first I was thrilled. Nothing would ever make up for the loss of my dear parents, but my hero, my uncle James, would help ease the pain. Even when Janetta became tense on the day of his arrival, and the staff were tight-lipped and whispering, I suspected nothing. In fact I had this romantic notion that Janetta and James would fall in love, marry, and live here with me forever.*'

'That would have been a nice love story,' sighed Susy.

'Now you're adding your own bits,' I snorted. 'This isn't some stupid novel, it's the real thing.'

'*The changes began within a week of his arrival. First of all I was withdrawn from school because James said I shouldn't be mixing with the village children. I wouldn't have a governess. I insisted that Janetta could give me lessons. A room upstairs was given over as our classroom. That room was to become a refuge for us both to escape from the drunken arrogance of this man who was trying to take over my father's estate.*

'*At nights I could hear the raised voices of Janetta and James as they argued. It always ended with doors slamming. One afternoon,* while *Janetta* and I were playing the piano, *James* barged into our room. He was drunk. *Janetta* was furious. She asked him to leave. He flopped into an armchair and put his feet on the coffee table. He'd been out riding, and his spurs scratched the polished surface. He just laughed and took out a silver hip-flask – it was Papa's. The smell of whiskey overpowered the scent of lavender potpourri on the piano.

'*Janetta* asked again that he leave. He raised his arm and pointed at her, told her he was tired of her looking at him with disdain. Then came the bombshell. He told her to pack her bags and leave. Now it was my turn to be furious. But no matter how I fumed, he just ignored me. And then *Janetta* said that she was all I had left since he'd forbidden my friends from calling and that she wouldn't leave me. My friends had been forbidden to call! I had thought that they'd abandoned me.

'Then *James* went on about being the legal inheritor of Heather Grange and that he'd take what was rightfully his. I didn't understand what he was saying. But *Janetta* told him he was entitled to nothing, that he was not a blood relation of the Smythes. Not a blood relation! At that I put my hands over my ears. I didn't want to hear any more of this awful talk. I jumped when I heard the chair being scraped back. *James* rose angrily and towered over a frightened

80

*but resolute Janetta, knocking over Mama's
pretty standard lamp. Mama had had that lamp
especially made by our local ironmonger to
celebrate Papa's thirty-fifth birthday.*

'*That made me really angry. I shouted at
James to stop, to go away and leave us in peace.
But James turned on me.*'

I paused. 'This is where it gets compli-
cated,' I said as I glanced at the words ahead.
'To cut a long story short, it seems Maria's
grandparents had a maid who became
pregnant by a farm-hand. He absconded.
Maria's grandparents took pity on the girl
and helped her to bring up the kid.'

'The kid being James,' said Susy.

I nodded and went on, putting things in
my own words because Maria's were full of
the sad stuff that Susy didn't want to hear.

'The maid died and they took in the child.
Even gave him their name. Then they had
their own son, years later...'

'That was Alfred – Maria's father,' Susy
interrupted.

I nodded again and digested the next bit.
'They brought up the two kids as if they were
brothers. James joined the British army at
seventeen – Alfred was just six. They never
saw much of him after that. He made a mess
of his life. Thrown out of the army, gambling
debts, fighting, all that sort of stuff. The old

man paid some of the debts. But gradually James just cut himself off from the family altogether. Came back for the parents' funerals, but hopped off again on his travels. He was left money in the old man's will. Gambled and drank it all away.'

'And then came after the whole estate,' Susy interrupted. 'The pig.'

'Coming back like that out of the blue,' I said. 'Thought he'd latch on to an easy number by being all brotherly. '

'In my eye!' said Susy. 'Go on.'

'Janetta accused James of forging adoption papers after Grandpa died. She said that Papa never thought to find out if they were legal. He trusted James.'

'Big eejit,' put in Susy. 'If he'd checked then, none of this would have happened. But how come Janetta knew that?'

'Seems the people in the village knew,' I said. 'And Maria's mother. But Alfred would never listen to a word against James … cripes!' I exclaimed as I read on.

'What do you mean "cripes"?' asked Susy.

'Now it gets hairy... James turned on Janetta and grabbed her by the throat!'

Susy's hand went to her mouth. 'He killed her!' she said.

'No. Maria ran to the window and scream-ed for Jake.'

'The gardener!' exclaimed Susy. 'That's who the man in the drawing was.'

'Must be,' I said. 'Anyway, she shouted for him.'

Jake rushed in. He swung the shovel he still had in his hand and struck James on the back. As James turned around, one of his stirrups caught on the lamp he'd knocked and he fell backwards. I can still see it, as if it was in slow motion, James caught off-balance and falling, his red face twisted with bitter resentment. With a crack, his head hit off the brass fender before the fire and he lay very still.

'I screamed again when I saw the blood begin to ooze from his ear. Janetta had one hand on her throat, with the other she pulled me to her as I began to sob hysterically. Jake got down on one knee and felt for a pulse. He tried James's neck, then his wrist, then his neck again. There wasn't one. James was dead.'

'Oh God!' Susy murmured.

Janetta sank into a chair. Jake just stood there as if he couldn't believe what had happened. I remember the sound of the clock ticking and the birds singing in the trees outside – all these normal things going on while in here the most awful horror had just taken place.'

'He deserved it,' said Susy. 'He'd have killed Janetta.'

'Who knows?' I replied. 'With her and the

parents out of the way he would only have had to deal with the kid. It says here that he'd intended to become executor of the estate.'

'What does that mean?' Susy asked.

'I think it means that he'd be in charge of everything until Maria would be old enough. Probably sell off stuff in her name. Bits of land, valuable antiques and things.'

'He'd never have got away with it.'

'You want to bet?' I laughed. 'That was way back in the thirties. Even now, in the twenty-first century, and in spite of all the sophisticated technology, there are still loads of people getting away with all sorts of frauds. Think about it.'

'Suppose so,' said Susy, picking idly at the wood grain on the table. 'Anyway, what happened? Did they get done for murder, Janetta and Jake?'

11

'Susy, it was an accident,' I pointed out as I looked to see how many pages were left. 'Not much more to go. Listen to the last bit.'

'Jake kept moaning that he'd be found guilty of murder. Janetta kept telling him it was an accident and that she'd hire the best lawyers. But the more they talked, the more obvious it became that Jake would have to stand trial. He feared for what his family would suffer when all of this came out.'

'Go on,' said Susy impatiently.

'Wait,' I said as I read on. 'Cripes! Janetta had Jake bury the creep in the garden!'

'What?'

I nodded.

'Janetta said that James had been a wanderer all his life, that people would simply think he'd gone on his travels again. She said he wouldn't be missed.'

'Too right,' muttered Susy.

'Sshh,' I said. 'Let me go on.'

'Jake was shaking his head, but Janetta was very firm. She said we'd bury him in the garden, as casually as if she was talking about a dead cat, and that nobody need ever know. Then she

went on to say that she and I would go away to France, her homeland. People would think that the three of us had gone away together. It would seem like we were leaving the house because it was too sad to stay here without my parents. And so it was decided. Jake buried James Smythe in the orchard.'

'In the orchard!' exclaimed Susy. 'I'll never eat another apple.'

'Janetta and I packed everything belonging to him, including personal papers, into the big chest he'd brought with him. When Janetta said that there was no way she would take that chest with us on our journey, Jake came up with the idea of storing it in the attic and then sealing it off.'

'Ha!' I broke off. 'Could *that* be Mrs Powell's "chest" – and is *that* why that attic window was sealed off… She goes on to say how sad she is at leaving the house.'

'Jake has told us not to worry. He will look after things and tell the village that we'd all gone abroad for good, just like we'd arranged. Later, Janetta says, she will get an agent to organise the sale of the furniture. Apart from personal things belonging to the family, there's nothing that we want to take with us. James's chest is packed. When we've left, Jake will take it to the attic and seal it away. Janetta has also said that she will arrange, through solicitors, to sell the furniture and set the land until I come of age. At

86

that stage I can sell it if I want to. But the house and its five acres of garden will never be sold. It will remain there as a tomb for an evil man. I have given Jake all my sketchbooks. I don't want to take with me any reminders of this place which changed from a happy home to a place of evil.'

'So she gave Jake the sketchbooks! But who put them up for sale?'

I shrugged. 'Dunno. Look, I'm on the last page.'

'If you are reading this, then you have found the sealed sketchbook cover. And you are wondering why I've put this diary there. I'm hoping that, by writing the full account of what happened in this house, I can leave all the misery of recent times behind me.

'I know there will be rumours caused by our disappearance, but to stay here would, as Janetta says, put us in a position of living under a shadow too awful to contemplate. Signed, Maria Smythe.'

'That's it then?' said Susy.

The last page was blank. 'That's it.'

'Whew! Is that a hairy story or what!' Susy exclaimed.

'Where do we go from here?' I wondered.

We both jumped out of our skulls when the phone rang. Susy looked at me. 'Half-four. Who'd be ringing at this hour?'

'Only one way to find out,' I said as I got up to answer it, trying not to think about my parents and car accidents. Or about a spook with a mobile phone.

'Arty?' a voice asked. 'It's Cathleen. I'm so sorry to disturb you at this hour. Is your mother there? It's about Mrs Powell.'

I swallowed hard. 'Is she...?' I was too scared to finish the question, a rush of guilt and concern flooding into my brain.

'She's very ill,' Cathleen went on.

'I'm afraid Mum's not here,' I said. 'She and Dad won't be back until tomorrow – I mean later today.'

There was a pause. Then Cathleen spoke again. 'I really just wanted your parents' permission to ask if you could come here.'

'Me?'

'Yes. It's you Mrs Powell keeps asking for. Could you come? I kept telling her we'd fetch you in the morning, but she insists that she wants you now. I'm afraid if we leave it that it will be too late. You know, I'd never forgive myself if anything happened and I hadn't granted her that one request. For the past few hours she's been in a terrible way. We'll send a car for you. But I'll understand perfectly if you decide not to come. It's a lot to ask a young boy ...'

'Of course I'll come,' I put in. 'Are you

sure it was me she was asking for?'

'Over and over. At first we thought she was just rambling, but she keeps calling for you.'

'I'll be ready,' I said. I liked Cathleen. She was Mrs Powell's favourite nurse.

'What was that all about?' asked Susy when I put down the phone. When I told her, she asked, 'And are you going?'

'Of course I'm going. What else can I do?'

'I wonder why she wants you,' went on Susy. 'Do you think it's anything to do with ... all that stuff she was trying to tell you?'

I took a deep breath as I weighed that up. I hoped it was just my charming personality that the old lady wanted.

Susy insisted on coming too. Well, there was no way she was going to stay in the house by herself. Not after what we'd been through.

Cathleen put her hand on my shoulder before we went into Mrs Powell's room.

'Are you sure you don't mind doing this, Arty?' she asked.

I steadied myself. 'I'll be okay,' I said. Well, that wasn't really how I felt, but what choice had I but to fib? Cathleen opened the door and led me in. The room was dim. I hadn't expected fairy lights and streamers, but this scene was even more depressing than I'd anticipated. Mrs Powell was lying flat on the bed. She was as still as death.

'Mrs Powell,' said Cathleen gently. 'It's Arty. I've brought Arty to see you.'

There was a slight movement from the bed. Good. She hadn't passed into the blue yonder.

'Arty,' she said weakly.

Cathleen gave me a slight push in the direction of the bed. Mrs Powell held out a bony hand. It felt like I was holding a dead bird. With her other hand, Mrs Powell indicated to Cathleen that she should leave.

'Hi,' I said.

'Hi,' she smiled and closed her eyes.

Silence.

Was this it? Was I just supposed to stay here clutching her bony hand until she decided I could be released back to civilisation? Suddenly her eyes opened. There was nothing feeble about her stare. She looked intently at me, as if she could see right into my soul. I dropped the dead-bird hand and backed away.

'Arty,' she beckoned. I approached her gingerly. Her face was bright and very much alive. This was the old Mrs Powell that I knew so well. I sat down on the bed and took her hand again.

'That house, Arty,' she began, giving me her direct look. 'I have to tell you about that house.'

12

Susy was sitting with Cathleen and drinking tea from a plastic cup when I came out. She looked at me expectantly, but I said nothing. Mainly because my jaws were welded together with fear. While Cathleen went to check on the old lady, Susy leaned over.

'Well?' she said.

'Tell you in a few minutes,' I muttered.

'Thanks, Arty,' said Cathleen, gently closing Mrs Powell's door. 'Whatever you said to her, she's much more peaceful now.'

It's not what I'd said to her, I wanted to scream. *It's what she offloaded on to me.*

But I just nodded and got into the car after Susy. On the way home I stared straight ahead, ignoring Susy as she pulled at my sweatshirt. Now and then the driver, who doubled as the bouncer at the Home, looked at me in the mirror and tried to make inane conversation. I let Susy do all the answering to questions about the holidays and telly programmes, the usual sort of stuff that adults engage in when they don't know what to say to young people.

'Are you going to tell me what went on or

what?' Susy said angrily when we got home.

It was still quite dark, which made me wish I'd left the hall light on.

'Susy,' I said. 'We have to go back.'

'Where?' She peered at me in the gloom.

'To the Grange. We have to go back to Heather Grange.'

That struck a chord. Susy backed away and looked at me with horror.

'What do you mean? What are you talking about, Arty? Are you winding me up?'

'I wish I was,' I sighed wearily. 'I wish more than anything I *was* winding you up.'

Susy looked at me anxiously. 'You look like death,' she said. 'I'll make some tea.'

I shook my head. 'Couldn't drink it.'

'Well, I'm making it anyway. People always make tea when there's a crisis. Is this a crisis, Arty?'

I nodded.

'Are you going to tell me about it?' she went on, as she filled the kettle.

Where to begin? My brain was still on a scary roller-coaster between real life and the edge of a chilling abyss.

'That James was a bad lot,' I said.

'We know that,' retorted Susy. 'For starters he tried to strangle Janetta.'

'That's not the worst of it,' I went on.

'There's worse?' she asked.

'It's him – he's the one who's been putting us through all this spooky stuff. He's far more dangerous dead than he ever was alive.'

'Get away! I don't believe it.'

'You'd better believe it,' I said miserably.

And so I told Susy about my bizarre conversation with Mrs Powell.

'She wasn't very clear,' I began. 'She wandered a lot. Bits of what she said were garbled and didn't make any sense. She's been having awful nightmares.'

'Nightmares? Is that all? There's nothing odd about nightmares.'

I shook my head. 'You don't understand. These were nightmares so real that, each time she came to, it was like she'd been in another existence. And each time she could feel her life slipping farther and farther away. That spirit of James is haunting her mind.'

I paused. 'It's trying to kill her.'

Susy gasped. 'Oh Arty! What's going on?'

'That's why we have to go back to the Grange,' I said. 'Now! Mrs Powell said that if this...this thing enters her mind once more, she'll die. She was definite about that. Then she said a very strange thing. That if she died, an awful mystery would die with her.'

'Mystery? What kind of mystery?'

'I don't know,' I replied. 'But there's

worse.' I looked at her, wondering how she'd take the next bit of information.

'Go on,' she said.

I said shakily, 'She said that if she dies, then that evil force will haunt us for the rest of *our* lives.'

Susy's face whitened. She drew back from the table, almost dropping her mug.

'Why, Arty? Why would that happen?'

'It's to do with the sketches we have,' I said. 'The sketches of the Grange.'

'I still don't understand,' Susy began.

'There's something in the attic that he wants to prevent anyone from finding,' I said. 'That's why he's been haunting us. When we found those sketches – the ones of the house before the attic was covered up – we opened up a whole chapter of evil.'

'What do you mean?'

I told her about the time I'd been looking at one of those sketches and how some unseen force had tried to tear it from my hand.

'And the time we were in the Grange. Remember?' Susy nodded. 'I had it in my back pocket. It was *that* the force was after. It tore my jeans to get at it. I never knew the meaning of the word scared until then.'

'What about the girl in the blue dress?' said Susy. 'The one we think is Maria.'

'She was protecting those drawings! She's

the one who put that mark on the roof of the house.'

'She wanted to make sure we'd notice that cover-up,' put in Susy. 'She wants us to go to that attic too. It's to do with her!'

'It is,' I agreed. 'It's all tied up with her.'

Outside, the first streak of dawn turned the kitchen window from navy blue to grey. Neither of us spoke for a few moments. No sound except for the clinking of Susy's spoon against the mug.

'Then Mrs Powell went on about that chest again,' I went on.

'Chest? The one in the diary! James's chest!'

'Yes, that was what she meant. The chest in that sealed attic at the Grange. There's a package in it which we have to get and give to Mrs Powell. Unless we do, she'll die – which means we'll be chased by that spook for the rest of our lives.'

'Cripes! What's in this package?'

I shrugged. 'Don't know. Mrs Powell doesn't know either. She just knows that it's the key to this whole weird scene. Whatever's in that package there, the evil spook is trying to make sure no one finds it. Let's go. We have to do this, Susy.'

Susy nodded. I took a torch from the dresser and we went out to get our bikes. On the way I told Susy the rest of Mrs Powell's struggling conversation. How she had known about the package, but didn't know what it contained.

'What has *she* to do with all this?' asked Susy. 'How come she knows so much?'

'She lived here years and years ago,' I said. 'Maybe she knew the family.'

'She must have been a friend of Maria's. That'd make sense. She would have been around the same age. Remember that creep James stopped all Maria's friends from calling? Maria must have written to her after she went away.'

'Makes sense,' I agreed. 'But Mrs Powell kept insisting that all this stuff won't cease until we get that package.'

'How will we know it, this package? There's bound to be loads of stuff in there.'

'It's the only package of papers,' I replied.

'Why didn't Mrs Powell look for it when she came back? Why leave it until now?'

'Maybe it only became urgent when she started having nightmares.' I paused. 'For the last couple of days those nightmares seem to have taken her over. She can't control them like she used to. They're stronger now.'

Susy thought for a moment. Then she looked at me. 'Are you thinking what I'm thinking? Could someone be sending her a message through those nightmares?'

I nodded. 'She's only had them since I started asking her about the house.'

'That's true.'

That gave us food for thought so deep we could smother in it.

There was a morning mist over the fields as we cycled along the deserted road. When we came to the rusting gate we dismounted and looked at one another with dread.

'Better go and get this over with,' said Susy, voice not quite steady.

Once more we made our way along the overgrown avenue, the swish of our feet on the dew-wet grass the only sound in the early morning. When we came within sight of the house Susy stopped. 'Are you sure about this, Arty?' she said nervously. 'That it's not just the wild talk of an old woman gone ga-ga. Maybe she's just imagining all this.'

I gave her a scathing glance. 'Susy,' I said. 'All that stuff we've been going through ever since you bought those cruddy sketchbooks, did we imagine it? Are you saying that we're going ga-ga too? I think not. Come on.'

'Why us?' Susy sounded really scared. 'Why couldn't she have told someone else to get that stupid package?'

'Because we're the ones who worked out the bit about the concealed attic,' I replied.

'We're the ones with the sketches. And we're the ones who'll draw this evil creep on us if we don't see this through.'

'We don't know that for certain,' said Susy. She was still scared.

'You know it's true,' I retorted. 'We're stuck in this and there's only one way out. You with me or not?' I strode ahead with a show of bravado that disguised the bright streak of cowardice that was flashing in my mushy brain.

Susy sighed miserably and, to my great relief, came after me. Together we edged our way to the broken panel in the front door. With every muscle tensed, I eased my way through and waited for Susy. Her white face stood out like a mask in the gloomy hall.

'Let's find that cruddy attic and get this finished,' she said.

The cold in that hall was something more than just the cold of the dawn. It was a cold that gripped with fingers of ice. A cold that whispered of old tombs and dark places. And fear. Unspeakable fear.

13

Staying very close to each other, following the yellow beam from the torch, we eased our way up the dusty stairs. And I really mean 'eased'. Whenever a step creaked, we froze. We made it to the landing and breathed deeply. Well, fairly deeply.

'So far so good,' whispered Susy.

I put my finger to my lips, too scared to mutter a quiet 'sshh'. We shuffled along a dark corridor towards a line of closed doors.

'Get out the sketch,' whispered Susy, stopping outside the first door. 'We need to find out which room is under that attic window.'

As I reached into my back pocket, the sudden screaming took us both unawares. Of course we were braced for some sort of spookiness, but that scream was beyond any sound we'd ever imagined. A tortured, desperate sound that began back at the top of the stairs and stormed along the corridor. We put our hands over our ears and sank to the floor. I could feel the sketch in my hand being pulled. I thrust it into my shirt and crossed my arms over it. I was being dragged along the corridor.

'Susy!' I yelled.

'It's the sketch,' shouted Susy. 'Let it go.'

'No,' I retorted.

'Let it go!' she ordered.

I had no choice. I was being dragged to the darkest part of the corridor, my heart not sure whether to beat like a machine-gun or stop altogether. I took out the sketch and ripped it to bits. There was a thundering howl that made me clap my hands over my ears again. And then nothing. The silence seemed altogether more deadly.

'You okay?' said Susy in a loud whisper.

I had my hand on my heart to try and steady it. 'Just about,' I gasped.

'It's gone,' Susy went on.

'Yeah, so's the sketch. Can you remember which window the attic was over? I can't.'

'All the times we looked at that sketch,' complained Susy. 'Surely you noticed which window it was.'

'Well, did *you*?' I asked.

'I think it might be the third window from the left,' Susy said doubtfully. 'Or the fourth.'

'That's just great.'

I started to launch into a long moan about how useless this search was when Susy fixed me with one of her steely glares.

'Whinging won't solve anything. We'll just have to search without the sketch. Come on, let's try the third door before...'

She didn't finish, but I knew she meant before that force would return. We pushed through to a dim, shuttered room. Tatty curtains flapped gently in the breeze from a broken window. There was a cast-iron lampstand with a broken shade lying in one corner – just the sort of junk Mum and Dad would have jumped at. Mum and Dad! I swallowed hard and tried not to think of home and parents in case I became a blubbering idiot.

Susy had gone ahead of me and was already tap-tapping at the panels on one wall. Through the slots in the shutters we could see the first fingers of blue dawn. We went about like two mad things, tapping for a hollow sound. No luck.

'All these stupid walls are solid,' said Susy. 'There's no sign of a covered-up door.'

She broke off and froze, staring at me with horror-filled eyes as that low whistle cut into the silence of the dawn. A low whistle that raised itself to a screaming crescendo as it swept along the corridor, coming towards this room. Hello God, I prayed inside my head. Are you receiving me? Take me quietly and painlessly before this thing shatters every

101

nerve in my body.

'Quick, hide!' hissed Susy.

'What good will that do...?' I began. But Susy shone the torch at the massive fireplace.

'In there,' she said, dragging me towards one of the cupboards that were on either side. We fell through, just as the awful sound stopped. Had it gone? We squatted down inside the musty cupboard and pulled the double doors shut.

'Turn off the torch,' I whispered. The sudden darkness prompted us to squeeze even closer together. It was suffocating in that cramped space, but we were too scared to breathe so there wasn't much call for air going in and out of our lungs.

We both leapt when the door to the room crashed open. I shut my eyes and waited for something to seek out Susy and me. But nothing came into the room.

We could just sense the awful presence poised at the door. We waited for a moment to see if it was recharging its batteries for another onslaught. Nothing. The ominous atmosphere lifted. Susy nudged me.

'That... thing is dead-set on stopping us from finding whatever is in the attic.'

'I know,' I whispered back. 'And as far as I'm concerned it's succeeding. We can't go on like this, Susy. Any attempt we make to find that attic will get the same treatment. I'm for calling it a day.'

Susy's face loomed closer to mine. Her eyes went through my head.

'What sort of a wimp are you?' she hissed. 'You've said yourself that if we don't get this mysterious package to Mrs Powell, then she'll die and this ghoul will be on our tails. No thank you very much. I'm not going to have an old lady's death on my conscience, nor a windy spook howling around my ears because I know about stuff that's hidden in an old attic.'

I sighed. 'You're right. I hate to admit it, but you're right. But what the blazes will we do? No matter what, that thing is going to come after us.'

'Then we'll have to split up,' said Susy.

I looked at her with disbelief. 'Split up? You can't mean that, Susy! Bad enough to try and cope together, but separated we'd go loopy with fright.'

'Speak for yourself,' retorted Susy. 'We'll have to get this thing over and done with. Just remember, Arty, no matter what screaming and howling it does, it can't kill us.'

'How do you know that?' I asked scornfully.

'Well, I've never heard of anyone being

killed by a ghost,' Susy replied lamely. 'Have you?'

'Susy,' I said with as much patience as I could muster, 'I've never met anyone who got so much as a whiff of a ghost, never mind ghostly gangsters who snuff out people.'

'Look,' went on Susy impatiently. 'Are we going to sit stuffed into this cupboard arguing about weirdos? We've got to get on with the search. That creep could come back any minute. Now, what about splitting up? It's the only way.'

I gulped. 'I suppose so. But how will we know where to look for the attic?'

'*Think*, Arty,' said Susy 'Where is this thing doing all its loudest carry-on?'

'The corridor,' I replied.

'Right on. The corridor. That has to mean that it's trying to stop us having a go out there. Makes sense anyway. Most houses like this have their attic doors in a corridor. You couldn't be going up and down to an attic through someone's bedroom, could you? In the sketch the attic window was over the third or fourth bedroom window, but that doesn't mean the entrance was in that room. It has to be the corridor.'

'Yes, but in our house the way to the attic is through a trapdoor outside the bathroom.'

Susy was shaking her head. 'In big old

houses like this there could be a sort of back staircase leading to an attic.'

'How do you know?'

'I just know, that's all. I've been thinking about it.'

How could she think logically at a time like this, I wondered?

'I hope you're right.'

'Arty, I'm always right.'

I let that pass. There wasn't time for sniping.

'I don't know if you're very mad or very brave,' I said as I climbed out of the cupboard.

Susy turned and looked at me with an intense determined look on her face.

'I bought those stupid sketchbooks,' she said. 'I got us into this and I'll get us out of it. I'm scared out of my mind, but I know we have to see this through.'

I gulped again because the last gulp had only been a throatful of air. We crossed the room and peered out into the corridor. Nothing, just darkness and silence. Susy nodded to me.

But before we put a foot in the corridor, the door suddenly slammed with a deafening thud.

'Locked!' cried Susy. 'It's locked us in!'

Together we pulled at the door, but it wouldn't budge. While I battled to get the door open, Susy ran to the window.

'It's too far,' she wailed. 'We'd end up in bits if we tried to jump, Arty.'

'We're going to end up in bits anyway,' I panted as I angrily kicked the door. 'We'll be found here years from now ...'

'Oh shut up, wimp,' said Susy. 'Come on, it's only a wooden door, for heaven's sake.'

'Susy, I don't know that I want to go out there,' I began. But before she could come back at me with another wimpish remark, the howling started again. Instinctively I curled up into a ball – I'll never again scoff at a hedgehog – and crouched against the wall, waiting for the onslaught. Outside the howling echoed up and down the corridor. Up and down. Not stopping at the door. I uncurled slightly and looked up at Susy. She put her finger to her lips.

'Sshh,' she said softly. 'Listen.'

'Voices,' I said in terrified amazement. 'Can you hear voices?'

14

I strained my ears, trying to hear what the voices were saying. Had someone come to rescue us? Had someone seen the bikes and come to investigate? My heart leapt. Whoever it was I'd put them right at the top of my Christmas card list. But then, with a sinking feeling, I realised that those voices didn't belong to any human. Ghostly voices arguing in and out of the airwaves, sounding like a radio with bad reception.

'What the hell, Susy?' I said.

'It's a woman's voice,' she said.

Over all the furore, we heard a click. The door opened a fraction. We looked at one another, undecided what to do.

'Maria,' said Susy. 'I bet it's Maria.'

'I don't want to go out there,' I said.

'We've got to,' said Susy, grabbing me. 'We've got to. Everything will be all right.'

Reluctantly I allowed myself to be towed into the dark corridor. The sounds had stopped, but there was still that ominous presence.

Susy turned to me. 'Remember our plan?'

'Remember what?'

'Splitting up,' hissed Susy. 'I'll go to one side, you take the other.'

'What!' I looked at her aghast. 'Susy, you can't leave me ...'

'Go on,' she said, giving me a push. I watched with horror as she made her way down the corridor. What was I to do?

My instinct was to curl up again, but I knew Susy was right. I braced myself. So well I might because the howling started again. With every nerve in a state of collapse, I made my way along the corridor. I was just at the next door when it hit me, like several bricks thrown against my back. Funny thing, but that made me angry.

'Get lost, creep!' I yelled. That helped a little. There's a lot to be said for shouting in times of gut-twisting fear. I knew this was the last try. If we didn't succeed this time then it was curtains for Mrs P. and Susy and me. I gritted my teeth and kept on tapping. I was barely conscious of Susy further along the corridor. The windy creep hesitated. Then it left me and swooped towards her. Her plan was working! Or was it? I heard her shouting, and back came our friend again.

I kicked at those panels, swearing whenever I heard the dull thud of solid wall. The next few minutes became a blur of my shouting and hammering and being buffetted against the wall by an angry unseen thing. Then Susy let out a triumphant yell.

'I think I have it!' she cried. 'Hollow.'

I fought my way to her and together we beat at the wooden panels. But the wood was strong and our hammering was as useful as trying to hack an iceberg with a toothpick.

'It's no use,' I gasped. 'Anyway how do we even know that this is the right...'

'Keep at it,' Susy interrupted. Then she ran back the way we'd come. Double panic. Was she scarpering and leaving me here to do battle? She ran into one of the rooms and reappeared wielding the cast-iron lampstand. But before she could reach me, she was pushed back.

'Arty!' she yelled. 'Here.' And, with that, she tossed the lampstand at me, almost amputating both my legs while she was at it. I grabbed it and swung it in desperation. At first nothing happened. I was practically sobbing as the force hit me again. By now Susy was beside me and we smashed at the wood.

When we heard the first splintering sound we cheered. There was a sound like a sigh and a gust of air hit us. It wasn't the only thing that hit us. We were being buffetted unmercifully.

'Oh God!' sobbed Susy with frustration. 'We can't take this much longer, Arty.'

I was about to agree when there was a flash of blue at the hole we'd made. The merest flash, but it was enough to stop that spook in its tracks. Without stopping to wonder why, we made one last desperate attempt at enlarging that hole. Then we made a gap big enough to get through. We didn't stop to look back at the furore that was going on behind us – not that we'd have seen anything anyway. I scrambled through and hauled Susy after me. 'Turn on the torch,' she gasped.

We were on a spiral staircase. This had to be the old entrance to the attic. Please let it be, I prayed. I couldn't take any more. We beat our way up those steps as if every demon from hell was after us. Well, one of them was anyway. Or would be shortly. The door at the top of the stairs loomed ahead.

I paused before turning the rusty handle.

'Go on,' said Susy. 'That thingy will be hotfooting it up here after us.'

As I turned the handle, a heartrending wail came from below.

I opened the door. We'd made it. After all that, we'd got here. I shone the torch around and there, in a corner, just as Mrs Powell had said, was the chest containing James's stuff.

Feverishly we opened it.

15

After we pulled the package of papers from the chest, we didn't delay. That furore was still going on downstairs.

'We'll never get back through that storm,' I whispered.

Susy took the torch and shone it around.

'What are you looking for?' I asked.

'An opening,' she replied. 'A door to the roof or something.'

'Yeah, that'd be real handy, Su. In your dreams…' I broke off.

The sound we'd been dreading was making its howling way up the spiral stairs. I shoved the package inside my sweatshirt and braced myself for the final showdown. But before the howling thing reached the top of the stairs, a blue flash swept past us and stopped at the far end of the attic. For one fleeting moment I could clearly see the girl from the auction, with her old-fashioned hair and her dress with frilly things down the front. And then she pointed. Just that. Susy grabbed me and dragged me towards the spot.

'I knew it,' she cried. 'A door.'

Without pausing to wonder where it led,

we began to push back the rusty bolt. It wouldn't budge. We both yelled when the howling sound stormed into the attic. Looking over my shoulder, I caught the terrified look on the spectral face of the girl. Just before she was swallowed up in the vortex of that angry force, she looked at me. A direct, familiar look. A look I knew well. And I knew then what had to be done! Why couldn't I have seen it before now? With a renewed onrush of adrenalin, I tackled that bolt.

'Susy!' I panted. 'We've no time to lose.'

'I know that,' she retorted.

'No,' I said, gritting my teeth. 'I really mean it. I *know* what this is all about.'

Panting and gasping, we pulled at the bolt with all our strength. At first, nothing. Just when I thought everything we'd been struggling for was about to be lost, there was a slight budge.

With a delightful clunk, it shot back.

'Quickly!' said Susy. 'Before it...'

'It won't,' I said. 'It's not after *us*.'

'What...?' Susy began. But before she could start asking questions, I hauled her through the door.

'Steps, Susy!' I cried out.

And so there were – the steps of a dilapidated fire-escape leading to the ground. We hurtled down those steps as if our lives depended on it. Which, of course, they did. Some of the steps were broken and we had to jump clear. We fell in a heap at the bottom, not quite believing that we were back in the fresh air. We didn't stop running until we reached the first fence, the one Mum had said that nobody dared pass. Only then did we turn to look back. There was nothing after us. Just as I suspected. There was absolutely no time to lose.

'Come on, Susy. We're out of here,' I cried, grabbing my bike and mounting it.

'Where are we going?' she called after me.

But I'd gone ahead. To try and explain to her would have cost valuable time. She caught up with me as I sped through the gates of the Home.

'Just what the blazes do you think you're doing?' she panted. 'It's too early in the morning. We won't be let in?

I ignored her and tried the front door.

'It's locked, you clown. I told you, it's too ...'

She broke off as I put my finger on the bell and kept it there. I was conscious of Susy backing away, ready for a quick getaway, but I didn't care. Only one thing mattered now. I sighed with relief when the door opened a bit. A very annoyed face peered out from the narrow gap.

'What do you think you're doing?' It was the bossy nurse who'd ejected me before. 'I thought I told you...'

'Please!' I said, trying to push the door. 'I've got to get in. It's Mrs Powell. I've got to see Mrs Powell.'

The door was pushed against me. 'Mrs Powell is very ill,' came the angry reply.

'I know. That's why I'm here. I know what's happening. You must let me see her.'

The face at the door reached boiling-point. 'I'll have the gardai on you,' said the nurse, 'if you ever come within yards of here again.'

She made to shut the door, but I jammed it with my foot. At that she yelled for the security man. He came running, pulling on his jacket. It wasn't the man who'd driven us home. At least he'd have known who we were.

'What's going on here?' he asked.

By now Susy was at my side again, tugging at my arm. 'Come on, Arty,' she said. 'We've no business here. Let's go home.'

I pulled away from her, dashed through the door, skipped past the startled nurse and neatly side-stepped the heavy. Along the corridor I raced. I was at the door of Mrs Powell's ward when they caught up with me.

'Right, you little hooligan,' snarled the

heavy, grabbing me by the arm. 'You want locking up, you do.'

I was no match for his brawny muscle and I felt myself being dragged away.

'Leave him alone,' said Susy. 'He knows what he's doing.'

'He knows what he's doing all right,' hissed the nurse. 'He's breaking in here, disturbing people...'

'You've got to listen to me,' I pleaded, clutching at the doorpost.

'Get the day security man,' the heavy ordered the nurse. 'I'll hold this fellow until he gets here. Little thug.'

I looked helplessly at Susy. Without stopping to wonder if I'd gone insane, she lit into the great lump of a man. He brushed her off as if she was an irritating fly. You don't do things like that to Susy, not even if you're built like a brick wall. With a mad cry, she sunk her teeth into his free hand. That did the trick. With a yell he let go of my arm, just long enough for me to get to the door. But it was already opening. With a cry of relief I saw that it was Cathleen.

She was frowning. 'What's going on here?' she asked. 'What's all the racket?'

'Cathleen!' I cried. 'Tell them. Tell them I've got to get to Mrs Powell. I know what's wrong with her. I'm the only one who can save her!'

Cathleen was shaking her head. 'Hush, Arty,' she whispered. 'It's... it's too late. She's in a coma. She's been worse than ever. It's like there's a storm inside her head. It's only a matter of minutes. I'm sorry.'

A storm inside her head! A cold feeling spread over me. 'No!' I protested. 'It's not too late! Not yet. Let me go in, Cathleen.'

A hand roughly grabbed me by the shoulder. 'I have him,' said the security man. 'He won't get away this time.'

Cathleen looked helpless. Was this it? Had Susy and I gone through hell to be thwarted at the very last minute?

'Let him in, Cathleen,' said Susy. 'He can help. I know he can.'

'You!' said the security man in a loud, hissing whisper as he pointed a finger at Susy. 'You get away right now or you'll be hauled to the nick along with this fellow.'

All the fight was gone from me now. I had no choice but to let this muscle-bound creep drag me away in his vice-like grip. Being hauled over the coals by the hospital authorities was nothing compared to what was going to befall Susy and me after Mrs Powell's death.

'Wait,' said Cathleen. 'He might be right,' she went on. 'Mrs Powell has been asking for him constantly. Even comatose, she was crying out his name. Let him go, Mick. I'll take responsibility.'

I let out a great sigh. Mick was slow to release me, looking doubtfully at Cathleen.

Reluctantly he let me go. I made straight for Mrs Powell's ward.

'Any trouble and you're mincemeat,' Mick called after me.

I could be mincemeat already, I thought as I looked at Mrs Powell's inert body. Was I too late? I rushed to her bedside and knelt beside her good ear – if it was still good that is.

'Mrs Powell,' I whispered urgently. 'I have it. I have the package. I can tell you what's in it.' I whipped it from under my sweatshirt and feverishly opened it. 'Please listen. You have to know.'

I could have wept with relief when her eyelashes fluttered. She was still alive! With a feeble wave, she indicated to the anxious group at the door that she wanted to be alone with me.

As Cathleen drew them away, she looked back at me and nodded before closing the door. I was so grateful for her trust. I opened out the package and spread the letters it contained on the bed, anxiously scanning them for a clue as to why it was so important for the spirit of James to prevent their contents becoming known to Mrs Powell. Then I found the letter which mattered.

As I read it aloud, Mrs Powell's eyes rolled and she gasped, pressing my hand with each gasp. The storm was indeed inside her head. And I knew then that I still had to do battle with James Smythe. But the creep was no match for my determination and Mrs Powell's last shred of feistiness.

'It was you, James Smythe!' she cried out. 'It was you who killed my parents!'

She collapsed back on to her pillow. I held my breath. Then she smiled.

'It's all over, Arty,' she said, opening her eyes and giving me that direct look. 'The nightmares are finished for good.'

There was a silence. Not an ominous silence like we'd experienced back at Heather Grange. It was the comforting silence of of a normal summer morning. Between us – two kids and an old woman – we had pulled the plug on James Murdering Creep Smythe.

'So, you'll be hanging around for that cheque from the president then?' I said.

Her laugh seemed to give extra brightness to the early morning sun.

16

'It's all over, Mrs Powell,' I whispered. 'It was you, wasn't it? The girl in the blue dress – that was you?'

She nodded. 'How did you suss that?'

'The way you look at me,' I replied. 'I'd know that look anywhere. That time in the attic. I knew then. I knew it was you. It all made sense. Your horrible bouts coincided with ours. And then I remembered that you didn't know what was in the package and that I had to get it to you before...'

'Before he'd finish me off and have the secret die with me,' smiled Mrs Powell.

I nodded.

She laughed gently, then sighed. 'One part of me wanted to stop you going there, Arty. You and Susy. But another part wanted this... this secret to be known, even though I didn't know that there was a greater, even worse, secret....' She lay back on to her pillow. 'Thank goodness it's all over,' she said. 'The nightmares are finished for good.'

'I didn't know live people could be ghosts,' said Susy, who had joined us.

Mrs Powell nodded slowly. 'When something so strong pulls you to the truth, the mind is capable of anything.'

'I thought that the girl was Maria, the girl who did the drawings,' Susy said with undisguised disappointment.

Mrs Powell smiled. 'But it was. I'm Maria Smythe. Yes, that's me.'

Susy and I gasped. Mrs Powell was the little girl who'd been through all the horrors in that diary! Neither of us said anything – we were gobsmacked.

'We thought you were just a friend of Maria's,' said Susy.

'No, I'm Maria,' Mrs Powell went on. 'I always knew that James's evil presence was there. That's why I would never allow the house to be sold, even though the land had been sold off to provide money for Janetta and me. I knew its dreadful secret would be a danger to whoever bought it. That house has haunted me for so long. I had hoped the secret of James would die with me, but when you found that old diary I knew that the time I'd been dreading had come. I knew that he would stop at nothing to prevent you from finding that package. That's why he tried to get the sketches, to stop anyone from finding out about the attic.'

'And the diary,' I put in.

'And my diary, which showed what a

callous crook he was. That would have pointed someone – you, as it happened – in the direction of the attic too, to find out the rest of his dreadful secret.'

'Did you not know, Mrs Powell?' asked Susy. 'Did you not know what was in it – in that package of letters?'

Mrs Powell shook her head. 'It all happened so quickly,' she said. 'After the... the accident, we just wanted to get away as quickly as possible. Everything belonging to that thug was put together and sealed away in the chest. It wasn't until I came back here that those haunting nightmares began to really take over my mind. Nightmares that centred around the package. Always that deep feeling about that package, as if someone from beyond wanted the truth to be known.'

'Someone?' said Susy. 'Janetta?'

Mrs Powell shrugged. 'Janetta? My parents? Who knows? I felt desperate. There was nothing I could do. And then, when you brought in the sketch and told me about the strange things that were happening, I realised that there was more to my nightmares than just an old woman's mind going odd. Especially when they got worse and nearly drove me to my grave.'

'I didn't know you owned the house,' I said. 'Mum didn't know either. You kept it a secret ever since you came back here, didn't you? That and your identity.'

She nodded. 'My solicitor knows who I am, but he's sworn to secrecy. And one other person...'

'But why?' cut in Susy. 'Why didn't you want anyone to know?'

'Because I still owned the house. I didn't want people hassling me to sell. I didn't want anyone asking questions. Better to leave things lie. Or so I thought.'

'Does anyone else know the story?' I cut in. 'About Jake and how he...?'

Mrs Powell snorted gently. 'Not likely. That secret has stayed with just three people through all those years – Janetta, Jake and me. I never even told my husband. I suppose it was a sort of selective amnesia. I shut it from my mind when we went away.'

'And now you know the truth,' I said.

Mrs Powell sighed and a look of sadness crossed her face. 'Now I know,' she said. 'The whole shocking truth.'

'Why did you try to stop us?' I asked. 'I still have the marks of your nails.'

'I was afraid for you. I didn't want you putting yourself in danger.... Were you very frightened?'

'Me? Scared?' I forced a laugh. 'As if!'

'Arty!' scoffed Susy.

'Yeah, you're right,' I said. 'I was scared out of my mind, I didn't know anyone could be so scared. But we knew that we had to see it through. Ever since there was all that weird stuff in the hall of the old house, I knew something needed sorting. Though I can't understand why that creep was trying to pull me in? Wouldn't you think he'd be trying to scare me away?'

Mrs Powell gave a shiver. 'You were already inside. With the sketch.'

'What do you mean?' asked Susy.

'You had the sketch, Arty. He had to have that sketch back, to safeguard against someone clever, like you two, trying to work out why the attic was sealed.'

'Followed me home, the creep,' I added.

'Hard to believe, isn't it?' said Mrs Powell. 'You were both very brave. And now it's finished.'

'No more weird stuff,' Susy said. 'Though I still don't know why you came back to a dead-end dump like Cashelderry.'

Mrs Powell lay back on her pillow. 'At my age, Susy, contentment is number one on the list of good things. I certainly have that in abundance. Up to the time of James Smythe I was so happy here. I knew and loved everyone in the village, as it was then, and felt loved in return. You never forget those childish, secure feelings. All the time I lived abroad, I always held dear the memories of Cashelderry. I had no children and, when my husband died a few years ago, I came back to see if I could find that contentment again.'

'Have you?' I asked. 'Have you found it?'

She smiled. 'In a different sort of way,' she replied. 'Yes.'

'What about Janetta?' Susy asked.

'She stayed with me, even after I married,' she said. 'Kind, faithful Janetta. She arranged the selling of the land and managed all my affairs until I was old enough to take care of myself. She was my constant companion in all the places that my husband and I lived. I nursed her through the cancer that killed her twenty years ago.We never mentioned our awful secret in all the years we were together. And, with Jake's passing, there was just me to carry it.'

'Did she know?' asked Susy. 'Janetta. Did she know what happened to your parents?'

Mrs Powell shrugged. 'She probably had her suspicions,' she said. 'But she never spoke of them. What would have been the point? My parents were dead and James was dead.' She folded her thin hands over the package of letters on her lap. The package that had almost cost Susy and me our lives.

'What about the chest?' asked Susy, giving a slight shiver.

Mrs Powell shrugged her bony shoulders. 'I've told Una and Frank that they can take any antiques that might be there, and to burn the rest. I don't even want to know what's in it – some silver personal things like brushes and cigarette cases – things like that, I seem to remember. We burnt his clothes. All I needed was this,' she tapped the bundle of letters. 'The greedy James,' she went on. 'I still find it hard to believe this letter from the man he hired to interfere with the brake cable that caused my parents to crash. He threatened to send an anonymous letter to the police unless James paid up. Bluff, of course. If he had told the police, he'd have involved himself. But his letter was enough to send James into a desperate temper that made him drink heavily. And that was how he was when he came barging in...' she stopped and gazed out of the window again.

'And the other letters?' asked Susy.

Mrs Powell looked at her.

'Other letters? Oh, they were from people he owed money to, gambling debts. Threats demanding he paid up. He was penniless and desperate. No wonder he wanted me out of the way. With his forged papers he'd have made a tidy sum from selling the estate.'

'No wonder he didn't want us to find that package,' I said. 'Murderer. Are you going to tell the police?'

Mrs Powell gazed out the window again. 'No,' she said eventually.

'Do you not want it to go on record that James murdered your parents?'

She shook her head. 'What would be the point, Arty? Why open a can of rotten worms after all this time? And Jake's action would be brought into it. No, I'm just happy that the truth is known. You are my special friends, you and Susy, and you know the true story. Sometime, when I'm gone, you can tell it. But not now. The last thing I'd want right now is people coming to ask me questions, raking up old pain. All right?'

I nodded. 'All right.'

She gave me that direct look again and handed me the package.

'Burn this,' she said. 'And the diary too.'

'But the whole truth is written in there!'

She reached over and tapped my head.

'The whole truth is in there,' she said. 'Burn this for me.'

'If you say so. I don't know why, though.'

'Just do it,' she said, sharpish.

'All right, all right. I'll burn it,' I said. 'By the way, Mrs Powell, what about the sketchbooks that Susy bought at the auction? They were your sketches, weren't they? Did you put them up for auction?'

She had closed her eyes again and was smiling. There were voices coming towards us. I looked up to see a smiling Cathleen.

'Cathleen,' smiled Mrs Powell. 'Cathleen looks after me very well, I'll have you know. Spoils me rotten.'

The look that passed between them hinted at a special bond.

'Susy bought the sketches,' added Mrs Powell.

Cathleen laughed. 'Grandad would be pleased,' she said.

Grandad? I looked at Mrs Powell.

'Cathleen's grandfather worked on my father's estate all those years ago,' she explained, as if she'd read my mind. 'She's the only other person who knows who I really am,' she added. 'It was Cathleen who put those sketches into the auction thinking they'd make a bit of money for me.' She reached out and took Cathleen's hand. 'Thought they might make enough to allow me to stay on at the retirement home.'

'Three quid!' put in Susy. 'I paid three quid. That wouldn't keep you in peanuts.'

Mrs Powell laughed. 'Yes,' she said. 'But now I've something better to sell.'

'Jake!' I interrupted her. 'Jake was Cathleen's grandfather!'

'How did you know that?' asked Cathleen. 'He died long before you were born.'

'You've told Cathleen ...?' I had blurted out the words before I realised I'd done so.

Mrs Powell frowned and shook her head slightly. So Cathleen didn't know of her grandfather's part in this story. Just as well, I thought. People can get pretty upset about ancestors who do superhero acts with shovels. Homicide doesn't go down well in ancestral records, even if it's done with the best of intentions.

'Told Cathleen what?' laughed Cathleen.

'That I think it's time I did sell Heather Grange,' laughed Mrs Powell. Nothing wrong with the old lady's reflexes, I thought, as she neatly skipped around the question. 'Yes, the time is just right now. I'll sell the place.' She looked at me and then at Susy, and winked. Well, she could do that now that James had been defeated and the house returned to its peaceful state.

'You'll get a fortune for the house and garden,' said Cathleen enthusiastically. 'I could never understand why you didn't sell it ages ago, Mrs Powell.'

'There was a pest to be got rid of,' I said. 'Susy and I saw it off the premises.'